HIGH HURDLES

Letting
Go

Books by Lauraine Snelling

Hawaiian Sunrise

RED RIVER OF THE NORTH

An Untamed Land	*The Reapers' Song*
A New Day Rising	*Tender Mercies*
A Land to Call Home	*Blessing in Disguise*

HIGH HURDLES

Olympic Dreams	*Storm Clouds*
DJ's Challenge	*Close Quarters*
Setting the Pace	*Moving Up*
Out of the Blue	*Letting Go*
Raising the Bar	

GOLDEN FILLY SERIES

The Race	*Shadow Over San Mateo*
Eagle's Wings	*Out of the Mist*
Go for the Glory	*Second Wind*
Kentucky Dreamer	*Close Call*
Call for Courage	*The Winner's Circle*

HIGH HURDLES

Letting
Go

LAURAINE SNELLING

BETHANY HOUSE PUBLISHERS
MINNEAPOLIS, MINNESOTA 55438

Published by Bethany House Publishers
A Ministry of Bethany Fellowship International
11400 Hampshire Avenue South
Minneapolis, Minnesota 55438
www.bethanyhouse.com

Printed in the United States of America by
Bethany Press International, Minneapolis, Minnesota 55438

Library of Congress Cataloging-in-Publication Data

Snelling, Lauraine.
    Letting go / by Lauraine Snelling.
      p. cm. — (High hurdles ; 8)
    SUMMARY: When almost overwhelmed with activities for the summer including horse shows, art classes, and a greeting card business, DJ talks with her Gran and learns to trust God.
    ISBN 0–7642–2036–5
    [1. Horses Fiction. 2. Christian life Fiction.]
I. Title. II. Series: Snelling, Lauraine. High hurdles ; bk. 8.
PZ7.S677 Le 1999
[Fic]—dc21   99–6450
                                                 CIP

To Pat Rushford,
friend and encourager
Thanks

LAURAINE SNELLING fell in love with horses by age five and never outgrew it. Her first pony, Polly, deserves a book of her own. Then there was Silver; Kit—who could easily have won the award for being the most ornery horse alive; a filly named Lisa; an asthmatic registered Quarter Horse called Rowdy; and Cimeron, who belonged to Lauraine's daughter, Marie. It is Cimeron who stars in *Tragedy on the Toutle*, Lauraine's first horse novel. All of the horses were characters, and all have joined the legions of horses who now live only in memory.

While there are no horses in Lauraine's life at the moment, she finds horses to hug in her research, and she dreams, like many of you, of owning one or three again. Perhaps a Percheron, a Peruvian Paso, a . . . well, you get the picture.

Lauraine lives in California with her husband, Wayne, basset hound, Woofer, and cockatiel, Bidley. Her two sons are grown and have dogs of their own; Lauraine and Wayne often dog-sit for their golden retriever granddogs. Besides writing, reading is one of her favorite pastimes.

1

"REVERSE, PLEASE, AND TROT."

Darla Jean Randall signaled her horse, Major, into the trot and began posting. She kept her shoulders and back straight, her eyes forward, and her total focus on her horse and the ring. Keeping herself from admiring her competition took real discipline.

You know they are lots prettier than Major. DJ, as she made sure everyone called her, tried to ignore the sarcastic little voice, too—the voice saying *nanar, nanar, nanar,* like kids teasing each other.

She wanted to pat Major's shoulder, but she knew better. They were in the show-ring, after all, a big *rated* show-ring, with expensive horses and riders looking to the big time.

Like her, except she lacked the expensive, flashy horse that would catch the judge's eye.

"Walk, please."

Major snorted when DJ sat down and tightened his reins. He'd rather canter. He'd rather jump. But they were doing flat classes because Bridget Sommersby, DJ's coach, said that's what they must do.

DJ could feel sweat trickling down her back and alongside her right eye. May in California could be hot, and today proved that point. Her mouth felt as though cotton balls had taken up residence.

"Line up, please."

Major did everything she asked to his very best. That's the kind of horse he was—all heart, but as Joe had said, "No class. An old police horse like Major doesn't need class." Major's heart, though, had taken them over a lot of jumps. Joe Crowder, or GJ as DJ had dubbed him, was her fairly new grandfather and had become one of her very best friends and champions.

Ears pricked forward, Major stood still as the judge gave him barely a moment of her time before she went on to the next horse and walked around him to view the animal from all sides.

DJ could feel her jaw tighten. *How rude.* To almost ignore them just because her horse wasn't a warmblood or hotshot something. Always sensitive to DJ's moods, Major shifted his weight from one foot to another.

The judge walked toward the announcer and handed him her paper. DJ knew for absolute certain that their number and name weren't on that piece of paper. Their third class of the day, this no-ribbon thing was getting to be a habit. A not-very-comfortable, hope-it-goes-away habit.

As the announcer read the winners' numbers and names, the rider would nudge his horse forward to take the ribbon and then trot out the gate, waving the ribbon to applause from the stands.

DJ used internal super glue to keep her smile in place as the winners filed by. Only two days earlier she'd been dancing on rooftops at the result of her hard work. Her algebra grade had gone from a D minus to a B at midterms. But here in this ring, hard work didn't seem to count. *You just keep that smile in place,* she ordered herself.

"The rest of the class is excused. Thank you for participating."

DJ managed to keep the smile on her face, patted Major's shoulder, and followed the others out the gate, all of them earning only a smattering of applause as if they weren't worth the effort.

Except for a group higher up in the bleachers on the right side of the arena. The few competing riders from Briones Riding Academy, where DJ rode, trained, and taught young kids to ride, whooped and hollered as if DJ and Major had taken the grand champion prize. DJ's family cheered, too. She could hear her two fathers—Brad Atwood, her biological father whom she'd learned of only months before, and Robert Crowder, her stepfather of only a few months—yelling above the rest. She fought the temptation to glance up into the audience. Was that her mother's voice?

The idea of *her* mother up there shouting widened DJ's smile. When she passed the gate, her grandfather was waiting for her.

"You did your best." His smile said her best was more than enough for him and was, in fact, all that counted.

"I know." She patted Major's neck and down his shoulder. The rangy bay pricked his ears and nodded as if this show and class were the best ever. "You big old sweetie, you just like showing off." If they had been alone and DJ wasn't dressed in her show clothes, she'd have thrown her arms around him and let him slobber in her ear with carrot breath. "One more down."

"That's my girl. The next one is Junior Hunter Over Fences, so you'll like that." Joe took Major's reins. "You go get something to eat, and I'll take care of him, okay?"

DJ dismounted. "Thanks. If my stomach rumbled any louder, we'd have been sent out for disrespectful noises." She removed her helmet and wished she could let her sun-streaked hair loose from the netted bun she wore at the base of her neck. She patted Major once again and strode up the stairs to her cheering section.

"Poor DJ," said one of the Double Bs, as she sometimes called her five-year-old twin brothers, his round face as long as he could make it.

"No ribbons," the other added. The two had a knack for finishing sentences for each other.

DJ tousled a head with each hand and took a seat next to Brad. His wife, Jackie, who competed in higher-level dressage, shrugged.

"You did your best and got more experience in the ring. That's what counts." She slipped her hand out of the crook of Brad's arm and leaned around him. "But if I'd been judging, that guy on the chestnut would *not* have taken first. His ego is so big I don't see how his horse can carry him."

"All flash and no substance," Brad added.

DJ smiled at their comments, then shook her head. "But he even stumbled."

"I know. That makes it even harder to handle." Jackie reached around her husband again, this time to pat DJ's hand. "That's politics for you."

They're just trying to make you feel better, her little voice insisted, but DJ didn't care. Their comments *did* make her feel better. Funny, but she felt bad more for Major than for herself.

"Thanks, you guys."

Robert patted her shoulder. "You handled that woman who kept crowding you really well. I was about to yell at her to mind her manners, but your mother put her hand over my mouth just in time."

DJ knew he'd picked up that crowding knowledge from Brad and Jackie, but the thought of her mother doing what he said made her giggle.

"You need food, I can tell." Lindy leaned forward. "You

want me to go get you something?"

"We's hungry, too," the twins said in unison.

"You guys are always hungry."

The boys nodded their heads and grinned at her teasing.

Robert shook his head. "Come on, troops. Let's go get the food. Lindy, you want a hot dog, hamburger, or whatever sandwich they have? DJ?" They all gave their orders, including Brad and Jackie, and the three started down the steps.

"You think you can remember all that without writing it down?" Lindy raised her voice enough for them to hear.

"Of course." Robert rolled his eyes and shook his head. "Women."

"You all better plan on eating whatever comes," Lindy warned those still sitting.

DJ felt trickles of joy in her heart region. This was *her* family, and they were all here at the show to root for her, to do whatever they could to make her day go better. Only Gran was missing. A last-minute request from an editor for changes needed on an illustration for a children's book kept her home. She'd groaned as loudly as DJ when the order came.

"Sorry, darlin', but they need to get to press with this right away," she'd said. Gran made her living as an illustrator of children's books and had won awards for her work.

"There'll be other shows," DJ had answered. *"Lots of other shows."*

But she missed Gran's quiet comfort. Gran could say more with a hand on DJ's shoulder than most people said in five minutes.

DJ ate her hot dog rather than the hamburger she'd ordered without saying anything but a thank-you. She did, however, wink at her mother and get a wink in return. BR—before Robert, as DJ tagged her life—her mother wouldn't have been at the horse show, let alone winked at her daughter. She'd have been working or fighting a migraine most likely. Gran said the change was due to Lindy's no longer having the pressure of providing for her family. DJ didn't care about the whys; she just enjoyed the results.

"See you later." DJ wiped her mouth with a napkin.

"Time to get ready again?"

DJ nodded. "This is my last one for this show, so Joe and I'll be home later. I want to watch Hilary. She's in the last class."

"You need some help?" Brad asked.

"Not really, but thanks."

After no ribbon in her last class of the day, DJ fought against the twinges of envy she felt when Hilary had to jump two extra rounds to place second in her class. She was competing against known riders, something that DJ wanted to be doing sooner than as a college student like Hilary.

She had to keep reminding herself that she was only a freshman in high school and had a long way to go on her ride toward the Olympics. Hilary had the same dream, both of them seeing themselves as members on the United States Equestrian Team—or USET, as the horse world called it—one day.

But if today was any indication, DJ had a lot farther to go than Hilary.

"So do you want to talk about why your chin is down around your ankles?" Bridget Sommersby, coach and friend, sat down beside DJ.

DJ straightened and smiled with what she hoped was a genuine smile. Bridget didn't tolerate pity parties. "I wasn't feeling sorry for myself, if that's what you mean. I was just thinking."

"It is hard to do your best against overwhelming competition, no?" Bridget had ridden on the French team years earlier before she retired from competition and opened the Briones Academy.

DJ nodded. "But I did it."

"Yes, you did. And Major did his best, too. Anyone could tell the two of you were having a good time over the jumps. And while you did not win, you made a good showing. Now we decide what you learned." She waited for DJ to answer.

"Today I learned that I would rather jump than do flat-work any day of the week."

"That is something new?" A quirked eyebrow made DJ grin.

"No, just a reminder. In the flat classes I learned that all the competitors aren't as nice as I'm used to and that you have to watch out for sneaky tactics. They can throw you off guard. Even Major didn't like it. Did you see his ears?"

Bridget nodded and waited again.

"Um, I learned that I can do something that I know is necessary whether I want to do it or not."

"Ah, that is the important lesson. In competition as in life, there are many things we have to do, like as you said, whether we want to or not. The one who can give her best in those situations has gained a life-long principle." Bridget turned to face DJ. "You will go far, *ma petite*. I know you will." She stood and rested a hand on DJ's shoulder. "Tomorrow you and Major will take a well-deserved rest. Monday we will work on equitation over fences."

"Thanks, Bridget." DJ knew she'd take that amazing compliment out often in the dark times ahead and use it to spur herself on. Getting a compliment from Bridget was better than a blue ribbon any day.

"She's right, you know." Brad sat down on her other

side. "Hope you don't mind that I eavesdropped."

"No, not at all. I feel like I should write down what she said and frame it." DJ stared after the slender figure with her blond hair swept back in a chignon rather than the usual leather clasp.

"You're fortunate to be working with someone of her caliber this early in your career."

"I know." She turned to look at her handsome father. "You see any things I should have done differently today?"

"Not really. Your riding is fine, and you kept your smile in place. As far as I see it, this was a judge's preference for expensive horseflesh. You're going to encounter that more and more." He shrugged. "That's just the way of the horse show world. But you got more experience today, and one can never place too much value on that."

DJ nodded.

"You'll get more experience when you ride for us." Jackie joined in the conversation. "I think that's what you need now, exposure and mileage." Brad and Jackie owned a ranch in Santa Rosa where they raised and showed world-renowned Arabians. They both stood. "You coming?"

"In a minute. I want to say good-bye to a couple of people." DJ nodded to the group of riders from Briones who sat farther up in the stands. As she climbed up using the seats as steps, she saw thunderclouds on Amy's forehead. The others didn't look much happier.

"What's up?"

Amy and Tony leaned forward, sending spear-throwing glances over their shoulders. "You see those two guys up there?" Amy hissed, her dark eyes flashing sparks.

DJ looked up to see two men sitting a couple of rows up, both watching the class entering the ring. "Sure, what of it?"

Tony Andrada shook his head and rolled his eyes. "I

wouldn't want to get on the wrong side of our friend here. She'd just chew you up and spit you out."

DJ had to grin. Amy *was* a true friend, that was for sure. "So what of them?"

Amy sat back and chewed on her bottom lip. "Maybe I shouldn't tell you. You'll just get mad, too."

"Amy!"

"Well . . ." She glanced over her shoulder again. "I heard them talking and then realized they were talking about you."

"Me? I don't know them." DJ sat down on the bench below her friends but facing them.

"Me neither, but they know your dad."

"Which? Robert or Brad?"

Amy gave her a *get real* look. "Brad, of course. This is a horse show, not a construction show. Anyway, the fat one said he didn't understand why *your father* didn't give you a decent horse to ride, with all the great horses he owns."

DJ glanced up in the stands. "Come on."

"No, he really said that," Tony added.

DJ could feel the slow boil begin down around her midsection.

2

UP TO NOW IT HAD BEEN a pretty good day. Sorta.

"I felt like punching him out," Amy hissed.

DJ could hear Gran's voice in her ear, as if she were standing right there with her arm around her granddaughter. Gran was a great one for quoting just the right Bible verse. *"And pray for those who spitefully use you."* DJ felt like praying for the jerks all right, praying with a two-by-four in hand. The nerve! Who gave them the right to judge Major and her dad and her?

She sent them a glare fit to burn bacon. She wanted to storm up the risers and give them both a big piece of her mind, a big *loud* piece of her mind. But then Gran would remind her that if she kept giving her mind away in pieces, what would she have left for herself? DJ slumped, all her anger going out with her air.

It wasn't Brad's fault he hadn't given her a better horse; it was hers. She was the stubborn one, wanting to show Major and not Herndon. But Major was *her* horse, her very first horse, and she'd bought him with money she'd earned herself. Herndon had been Jackie's earlier dressage horse until she bought a better one. Herndon loved to jump, and the new trainer Jackie hired for the big gelding said Herndon would make a better jumper than he had as a dressage mount.

So why didn't DJ take them up on their offer?

DJ shook her head. "I love showing Major. He gives his best all the time and reminds me to do the same."

Tony nodded. "I know what you mean. I had a real hard time letting go of my first horse, too. The trainer I had then found the horse I have now, and my father said it was time to go on or get off. Did I really want to go places in the jumping world, or did I want to have a good time riding in the local shows?"

DJ studied the young man with the southern accent who'd become her friend after a rocky start. "You too, huh?"

"I'm glad I don't have to worry about getting rid of Josh." Amy loved her half-Arab gelding like DJ loved Major. Since Amy rode Western, she'd come to the show to cheer for her friends. "But then, I have no desire to jump in the Olympics, either. Why can't we just have fun with our horses and not get dragged into the 'go for the gold' thing?"

DJ looked at her with one eyebrow arched to her hairline. "Amy, how can you say that? You know all I want is to jump on the USET."

"I know. Just glad it's your goal and not mine."

"And mine," Tony added.

"And Hilary's. With the three of us on the team, there won't be a lot of room for anyone else." DJ glanced up as the two men who'd been talking walked down past them. She didn't even glare at them, which made her feel a tug of pride. She sucked in a deep breath and let it out again, feeling a wave of exhaustion that threatened to swamp her. The yawn that followed it nearly cracked her jaw. "Well, I better get on down to the trailer. Joe most likely is ready to go, and I've been lazy, letting him do all the work."

"You know he loves it." Amy stretched her arms over

her head. "You guys coming to the Rosedale Western Show next week to cheer the rest of us on? Joe's entering Western Pleasure again, isn't he?"

"That and a cutting class. He says he still may scratch that one if he and Ranger aren't ready."

"If you wait until you think you're ready in this business, you'll stay home all the time." Tony got to his feet. "Since I don't have a grandfather taking care of my horse, I better get going, too. Hilary's dad should be back pretty soon and we'll get out of here. I can't wait until I have my own rig and don't have to depend on others for transporting my horses."

"Horses?" DJ gave him a questioning look.

Tony nodded. "I'm going to be trying out another horse. The owner wants me to show him for a while whether I buy him or not."

DJ and Amy swapped their secret *I'm impressed* look. Sometimes Tony sounded a lot older than a junior in high school. But then, since DJ and Amy were just finishing their freshman year, even a sophomore sounded a lot older, too.

DJ was just glad he'd gotten over his redneck ways and become a real member of the Briones Academy family. At first she hadn't thought that possible, not the way he had treated Hilary.

But as Gran said, anything was possible with God. And DJ *had* finally been able to pray for him.

She stood and, along with Amy, followed Tony down the stairs. DJ couldn't remember when she'd felt so tired. Unless, of course, it had been the weekend before. School, homework, riding every afternoon, and showing nearly every weekend didn't leave much time for catching up on lost Zs.

But she didn't dare tell her family that, not since they were all working so hard to help her.

DJ fell asleep in the cab of the pickup going home, even though Amy and Joe carried on a conversation. Well, they were talking the last she remembered.

"You okay, kid?" Joe asked her when he stopped the truck and trailer in the Briones parking lot.

DJ blinked and flinched a bit at Amy's dig in her ribs. "I . . . I guess. We're home already?"

Amy rolled her eyes and shook her head. "Not *all* of us snored our way home."

"I don't snore." Another yawn did its thing on her jaw. If this kept up, she'd have to go to the doctor to have it put back in place. She stumbled from the truck and watched as Joe and Amy lowered the ramp. While she knew she should be helping, she waited, then walked in to untie Major and back him out. Within minutes they had their horses fed and watered and the fresh manure tossed out of the stalls.

She barely stayed awake long enough to say good-bye to Amy when Joe dropped her off at the Yamamoto house, then drove back past the Academy to DJ's.

"You get a good night's sleep, kid, or you'll end up sick."

"I've got homework to do." DJ groaned at the thought.

"Right, and I plan to re-roof my house. I thought you got that done on Friday."

"Most of it." DJ gathered up her duffel and the garment bag that hung behind the seat. She leaned over and gave her grandfather a kiss on the cheek. "Thanks, GJ. You are one awesome grandfather. Give Gran a hug for me. I sure missed her today."

"Me too." Joe shook his head. "Her and her deadlines. Sometimes I wish she weren't so good at what she does."

"Joe!"

"I know, I know." He raised his hands in defense. "It's awful to admit I'm jealous of the time my wife spends on her illustrations, but I hate for her to miss out on things like your horse shows."

"And *your* horse shows?" DJ waggled an eyebrow.

"She better not!" His grin deepened the creases in his cheeks and around his eyes.

"See ya." DJ shook her head as she bailed out of the truck and slammed the door. Her feet felt as though she were wearing cement boots. She waved again as Joe tooted the horn, then dragged herself up the curving walk to the broad front entrance of her family's new home. Tonight that Jacuzzi in her bathroom would feel pure heavenly.

"We're out here," her mother called when Queenie tore through the house, barking her welcome home, then leaped at DJ's knees.

"Hi, girl, guess you're glad to see me, huh?" DJ bent low enough for a quick doggie kiss. She set down her bags to ruffle the bouncing black dog's ears and tell her how wonderful she was. Queenie did all in her power to return the favor.

"Daddy's making sundaes." The boys plowed to a stop in front of her. "How come you took so long? We been home forever." The twins always ran their sentences together, a trick DJ had yet to figure out.

Queenie ran circles around all of them, her toes scrabbling for a hold on the slate-tiled entrance.

"We gots fudge. What kind you want?"

"Fudge sounds great." DJ pasted a smile on her face. Dropping her bags on the bottom stair, she followed the dog and twins out to the deck off the kitchen–family room combination.

"Uh-oh, you look wiped." Robert leaned back in his seat. With one hand he pulled out the chair beside him and gestured for her to take it.

DJ nodded and sank into the cushioned comfort. "I slept most of the way home, I guess. At least, that's what

GJ and Amy said." She covered another monstrous yawn with the palm of her hand.

"You up for a sundae?"

"Yes, please." She put her arms around each boy as they leaned on the arms of her chair. "How're my favorite brothers?"

"We's your only brothers." The twins looked at each other as if she'd gone batty.

"I know. Good thing, huh?"

"Well, that could change." Lindy leaned forward, her elbows on the table.

DJ perked up at the tone of her mother's voice. "Okay, something's going on here, I can tell."

"You want the works?" Robert called from the kitchen.

"Yes, please." DJ kept her gaze on her mother's face.

"Well, Robert and I were wondering how you might like a younger brother or sister." Lindy glanced up as Robert laid a hand on her shoulder and set DJ's sundae in front of her.

Robert smiled down at his wife, then at DJ. "As in *much* younger." He took his seat again and handed DJ a napkin from the green wire rack that held plastic picnic forks and spoons, along with napkins and paper plates.

"So what are you saying?" DJ dug into the nuts and whipped cream that nearly hid the hot fudge dribbling down the sides. Her stomach seemed to bounce somewhere around her ankles. Surely they weren't going to say what she was thinking they were going to say.

For once, the boys were still enough that DJ could hear the birds chattering in the ancient oak tree that shaded the deck as they settled down for the night. Somewhere a sprinkler ratcheted water on a lawn. Queenie sighed as she settled down at DJ's feet, her jaw flat out on her front legs.

DJ licked the fudge from her spoon.

Robert took Lindy's hand and sheltered it between his

two bigger ones. "What your mother is trying to say is that we are expecting a baby before Christmas."

"A baby!" DJ thought her eyes might leap right out of her head.

She looked from her mother to Robert and back again. "Aren't you kind of . . . I mean . . ." Her tongue flubbed the words.

"Old, you mean?" Lindy arched an eyebrow.

"Well, ah . . . yes—ah . . . no, I mean." Her chin hit her chest. "M-o-m!"

Robert shook his head. "You should see your face. Where's the camera when you need it?"

"DJ, you okay?" Bobby and Billy leaned against her shoulders, peering up into her face.

DJ took several bites of her sundae to give herself time to think. *A baby! I've never lived in a house that had a baby. Isn't this a bit soon? What's the matter with them, anyhow? How neat to have a baby. A real live baby brother or sister. But I've already got two brothers, and I don't know what to do with them half the time.*

Robert and Lindy exchanged another one of their sappy looks.

"Mom, I know you don't know what it feels like to get kicked by a horse, but that's about how I feel right now." She shook her head. "You coulda warned me, you know. How am I supposed to react?"

"Happy is what we hoped for." Lindy sighed. "We'd talked about having a baby, but we just didn't think it would happen so soon."

DJ licked more fudge from her spoon. She wagged her jaw back and forth. Then nodded again. "I *am* happy, I think. Just shocked. A baby . . ." She looked at the two boys, who were now rolling on the redwood decking with the dog trying to lick their giggling faces. She could feel her eyes turn into monster-sized Cheerios. "What if you have *twins?"* Her voice squeaked on the last word.

"That's always a possibility." Robert tipped his head and winked at his wife. "But we won't know that for a while."

Lindy groaned. "Now, *that* would really be exciting."

"Oh, it's not so bad. Been there, done that, got the T-shirt."

"Easy for you to say. *You* won't be the one giving birth." Lindy punched her husband playfully on the shoulder.

DJ ate her ice cream with a million thoughts screaming through her head. Finally she nodded. "Good thing we got a bigger house."

"Right," Robert said. "And now maybe we can convince this woman here to quit her job and stay home with her family." He patted Lindy's middle. "Her increasing family."

"I'm thinking about it."

Two shocks in one night was a bit much, even for DJ.

"But . . . but you said . . ."

"I know, I said more times than I can count that now that I have my degree, I looked forward to new positions in my company. But . . ." She gave Robert a smile so full of love that DJ's eyes burned.

"But?" DJ prompted.

"But who knew we were going to be a family then?"

"God knew." Robert's quiet words sent a blanket of peace to settle over them all. Even the birds silenced.

God knew. DJ let the words replay in her head. *God knew*. Gran always said that, too. Was this another of those God's-will things? Guess a baby could indeed be a God-thing.

"Darla Jean, you look like you can hardly stay awake." This time her mother's use of her daughter's full name held no anger, only love.

DJ yawned. "Sorry, guess I am wiped." She pushed back her chair and picked up her empty dish and spoon. "A baby, huh? Cool." She dropped a kiss on her mother's cheek and started for the kitchen. Stopping in the arch of the French doors, she returned to the table and kissed Robert's cheek, too. "Way cool."

Was that sniffing she heard from behind her? *Way to go,* the little voice in her head said. She could feel it smiling.

But a few minutes later, sinking into the frothing Jacuzzi tub, DJ shook her head again. First Gran got married, then her mother got married. Her biological father showed up. She now had a family that included two brothers. They got a new house. So many changes. And now a baby was coming. Would the changes never end? Wait until she told Amy about this!

3

IF THIS WAS MORNING, why was it so dark?

You have to open your eyes, doofus. The little voice worked nearly as well as the alarm that had been yelling at her for . . . she squinted her almost-open eyes . . . twenty minutes! *Yikes!* DJ bailed out of bed and into the bathroom without her feet even touching the floor.

Flying through the kitchen a few minutes later, she grabbed a breakfast bar and a juice box just as she heard the Yamamoto car honk in the driveway. "Where's Mom?"

"She isn't feeling too hot this morning, so I took over," Robert answered.

DJ stopped in her rush. "Migraine?"

"Nope, morning sickness."

"Oh." She'd heard about that.

"See ya." She tapped each boy on the head with her juice box as she headed for the door.

"Good morning to you, too. Got your backpack?" Robert called after her. Robert would get the boys off to kindergarten on his way to whatever jobsite he was working on at the moment. Her stepfather owned a very successful construction company, which was why they had recently moved into a fantastic house with a soon-to-be barn for the soon-to-be ponies for the boys.

"It's by the door. Thanks." Nothing like a rush to get ready for school to get the old adrenaline pumping.

"Have a good Monday," Robert called.

"Bye, DJ," the twins chorused.

"You too. Bye." The closing door cut off any further answers.

"Sheesh." Amy rolled her eyes at DJ's flyaway hair as DJ slammed the car door. "You forget to set your alarm?"

"Nope, slept right through it." DJ clenched a scrunchie between her teeth and attacked her hair with the brush she'd stuffed in her backpack. Once the dark honey-blond strands were confined in a ponytail, she spritzed the sides of her head to keep any stray locks in place.

"Wait until you see the last roll of film I shot," Amy said. "Totally awesome pictures of those pinto babies we found. John says with this computer program we just got, I can add things like hats and banners and stuff to the photos. I can't wait."

"You know how to do all that already?"

"Not exactly. She's paying John with chores time to teach her." Mrs. Yamamoto looked in the rearview mirror to smile at the girls in the backseat. Amy's older brother, John, was a computer whiz and tired of helping the girls with their money-making schemes. Their growing card line, however, was becoming more than a harebrained idea, as he had referred to it in the past.

"Bummer."

"Yeah, if he has his way, he'll have me doing the dishes for the rest of my life."

"I think you're learning the programs mighty fast. Wish I did algebra the same way."

"Concentration helps."

"Don't I know it." DJ's algebra grade had gone from nearly flunking to a B at midterm. It was either pull it up or say good-bye to her Olympic dream until after high school.

"Ya know, now that I'm winning in that area of my life, I know I can conquer just about anything." DJ smoothed some gloss on her lips and rubbed them together.

"Yeah, well, school isn't over yet."

"Hey, I thought you were supposed to cheer me on. Isn't that what friends are for?"

"What I better do is call you every morning so we aren't late."

The two girls bailed out in front of the Acalanese High School, thanking the driver as their feet touched down on the sidewalk. One more month and school would be out. They wove their way through the crowd to their outside lockers and quickly swapped the books they'd need for the first class.

"You got your algebra done?"

"Did that Friday. Good thing because I fell asleep in the tub last night." DJ stuffed another book in her backpack. "Oh, Amy, you won't believe what's happening now."

"What?" Amy pulled her head out of her locker, where she was looking for something. "Uh-oh, you've got that look on your face."

DJ dropped her voice. "My mother is pregnant."

"A baby! You're going to have a baby?" Her squeal brought looks from the kids around them.

DJ could feel her face flame. "Not me, my mother!"

"I know that. But you never had a baby brother before."

"Or sister."

The warning bell buzzed their attention.

"How cool." Amy had three brothers and sisters and had made sure that DJ felt part of their family for all the years they'd known each other. "You okay about it?"

DJ nodded. "I guess. Mom and Robert sure are. He's trying to talk her into quitting work. Can you believe that?"

They followed the flow into the classroom and took their seats, so they couldn't continue their conversation.

DJ thought about Amy's comment while the homeroom teacher took roll. Was she okay, or was that the little green-eyed monster of jealousy that pricked her every once in a while? She had to keep reminding herself that things were different now. Her mother wasn't the sole breadwinner anymore and didn't always put the twins before her *real* daughter; it just seemed that way at times. DJ knew she'd prayed about feelings like this, but still, sometimes they came. Calling herself names about it didn't help, either.

She sighed. Sometimes her *I can do all things through Christ* verse got stretched. Or was it her that got stretched? She'd have to ask Gran about this.

"Miss Randall, would you like to join us?"

"Huh?" DJ looked up from her doodling on her notebook. Her face flamed hot enough to boil water. In fact, her brain felt like it was doing just that—boiling. "Sorry."

"Daydreaming can best be used at other times, all right?"

She nodded. If only she could crawl out of the room full of snickering kids and douse her face in the washroom sink.

At least the day didn't go downhill too far from then on. The high point? She got eight out of ten points on the algebra quiz. And she nearly had another problem done, so only one had been over her head. First thing had been a quick prayer for God to clear her mind and help her to do her best. Then she took Robert's coaching to heart. As he'd suggested, she sucked in a deep breath and focused all her attention on the problems, doing the easy ones first. When the day came that she got a perfect score on a test or quiz, she planned to frame the thing. Robert had promised her dinner at any restaurant she wanted.

Waiting for her grandfather to pick them up after

school, DJ picked at a piece of dead skin around her thumbnail. At least she now had fingernails—the urge to chew on them came only when she was freaking out, like in class this morning. "There oughta be a law about embarrassing your students."

"Get real." Amy slung her backpack off and set it on the concrete curb. "Boy, was your face red."

DJ put her hands on her cheeks. "I can still feel it. Worse'n any sunburn I ever had."

Joe pulled up in front of them and leaned across the pickup seat to open their door. "Your taxi awaits."

"Thanks, Mr. Crowder." Amy slammed the door behind them.

"*Mr. Crowder?*"

"Well, I figured a taxi driver needed a better name than GJ or Joe." Amy set her backpack on the floor.

"I'll take Captain."

"You can't, you're retired." DJ nudged her grandfather with her elbow. "How'd your lesson go with Ranger?"

"Ranger isn't the problem." Joe eased his way onto Pleasant Hill Road. He flexed his right arm. "If I ever learn to throw a rope, it'll be a miracle."

"Just don't go in for bulldogging, okay? Gran will have a heart attack for sure."

"I won't. These old bones couldn't stand that. In answer to your question, Mark said Ranger has all the right instincts. He just needs experience." Mark was a trainer who specialized in training cutting horses.

"And more training?"

"Uh-huh, but I got me a feeling it's going to take longer to train the rider than the horse."

DJ nudged Amy. "Is that a negative comment I just heard?"

Amy nodded. "I think we should tell Bridget. What is it she says?"

"Something about *I can do it*?" DJ and Amy made absolutely sure their faces matched in serious mode. They both leaned forward to look at Joe.

"All right, all right, I get the hint."

"Hint?" DJ's eyebrows disappeared into her hairline. "That was a *hint*? Wait until we hit him with *both* barrels."

"What got into the two of you? Picking on an old man like this?"

"*Old man!*" Now they sounded just like the twins, in perfect unison.

Joe dropped Amy off at her house, then took DJ home to change so they could get to the Academy as soon as possible. Even with the days getting longer, the time between school and bed rushed by with the speed of a supersonic jet. Today was DJ's solo jumping lesson, Wednesday was dressage, and Friday was group jumping with Tony and Hilary. On Tuesday she taught what she used to call her "girl's class," but now with Andrew Johnson in it, too, she had to come up with another name. Beginners sounded too babyish for the sharp kids she taught. And while the girls rode Western, Andrew rode English.

As soon as she walked into the barn, Andrew met her at the tack room. "Guess what!"

"What?" She turned to see the kind of grin she wasn't sure she'd ever see on this little boy who was working so hard to overcome his fear of horses.

"Mom is buying Bandit—for me!"

"Wow, that's awesome."

"It is pretty awesome." Mrs. Johnson, her arm still in a cast, stopped beside her son and laid her other hand on his shoulder. "Thanks to you. I talked to the McDougalls one afternoon. I thought of putting Andrew up on another pony, but that might set him back. They said they were thinking of selling Bandit since their youngest girl just isn't interested in horses, so . . ."

"He's mine now." Andrew stood a bit straighter and smiled up at DJ. "Now I have to take care of him, huh?"

"You sure do, tiger. The more time you spend with Bandit, the better friends you'll become."

"I'm going to ride him now."

"Just for fun, huh?"

The boy nodded. "Mom's new horse will be here soon, and my dad says he might get one. Then we can go riding up in Briones with you."

"Oh man, I haven't been up in Briones forever. Soon as school is out, we'll all take lunch up there."

"Joe too?"

"Joe too." *That grandfather of mine is becoming pretty popular around here,* DJ thought on her way to Major's stall. She looked over her shoulder to see Andrew talking to the tall man with square shoulders and a crew cut. Joe said that way his gray hair looked more blond.

Major nickered as soon as she turned the corner to the outside stalls. While this area had a roof, poles held it up instead of walls, and aluminum rails separated the stalls. Ranger had the stall next to Major's, so it made cleaning them and caring for the horses easier. Joe took care of them in the morning, and DJ usually did the evening shift.

When she didn't answer, Major cranked up the volume.

Laughing, DJ clamped her hands over her ears. "Hey, I heard you the first time." She held out both closed fists, and when he nosed one, she showed an empty palm. "Ha. Fooled you." He nosed the other and took his carrot piece off her palm with an extra whiskery twitch. Munching that, he rubbed his forehead on the front of her T-shirt and leaned into her to get a good ear rubbing. When she stopped, he nosed her cheek and blew in her face.

"Ah yes, carrot breath. Just what I wanted." DJ turned so he could drape his head over her shoulder, the better for her to stroke his face and forelock. When he sighed in con-

tentment, she giggled. "You big sweetie, I must be the luck-
iest girl in the whole wide world to have a horse like you."
The thought of what those two men had said the day before
flitted through her mind. "They just don't understand how
much I love you, that's all."

"Who doesn't understand?" Joe set a grooming bucket
down at her feet.

"Two guys above us on the bleachers yesterday. They
said it was a shame Brad didn't give me one of his horses
so I'd have a decent horse to ride." Saying the words again
made a red haze pass in front of her eyes.

"Don't let it get to you, kid. If that's the worst thing you
hear, you'll be fortunate."

"I know, but the nerve! They don't know me and Major."

"In a way, they gave you a compliment."

"How so?"

"They must have thought you were a good enough rider
to need a bet—" He cut off the word. "A . . . ah . . ." He
winked at her. "A blooded horse, that's it."

"Good thing you didn't say 'better.' " DJ gave Major one
last nose pat and opened the stall door. Slipping into the
stall, she took a brush in each hand and, starting on one
side, brushed down her horse's neck and shoulders.

"I gave him a good brushing this morning." Joe took the
hoof-pick and set to work on his own mount.

"That's okay. I think I do this as much for me as for him.
There's something about grooming a horse that settles me,
gets me ready for my class or something. I don't know,
maybe I just love the feel and smell and sound of horses."

"You forgot sight." Joe straightened and slapped
Ranger on the shoulder. "Stop that."

Continuing the rhythm of brushing, DJ looked over the
barrier. "What'd he do?"

"Tried to take a chunk out of my rear, not that I don't
have extra, but . . ."

"So cross-tie him." DJ hid her grin by leaning closer to Major. Cross-tying was good sense, but she didn't usually do it with Major, either. At least not in the stall here in their home barn. He loved grooming so much he stood like a rock. "After all, Ranger's just a kid."

"Yeah, and a smart aleck one at that."

"You about done with that pick?" she asked after a couple of quiet minutes. She took a cloth out of her back pocket and wiped down Major's face.

"Yep. Here." Joe passed the pick between the rails. He crossed his arms on the top bar. "You *are* going to have to have another horse, you know, and if you want to progress as fast as you can, it'll have to be soon."

DJ raised up from picking Major's off front hoof. "Don't say things like that in front of my friend here. You might hurt his feelings." But DJ knew it was *her* feelings she was more concerned about. How could she stand showing without Major?

4

"HOW'D YOUR LESSON GO?" Lindy turned from checking a pot on the stove.

"No lesson, just riding. We had a day off. Bridget asked if I'd like to jump Megs tomorrow. Said she needs some exercise and I need more experience on other horses." Megs was Bridget's retired competition horse that had earned her place of honor at the Academy. "Can Amy come for dinner so we can work on our cards tonight?"

"Sure. How's your homework?"

"I got eight out of ten in the algebra quiz."

"Good for you."

"Where are the boys?" The house seemed almost eerily quiet, except for Queenie, who leaped and licked and glued herself to DJ's leg as soon as she walked in the door.

"Next door." Lindy glanced at the clock. "They should be coming home in about ten minutes. Robert will be late—he's got to finalize some blueprints. The table is all set and . . ." She covered the pan she'd been stirring and turned to DJ. "Other than that, how've you been today?"

"Okay." She told about the face-burning session in homeroom.

Lindy laughed and shook her head. "Boy, does that remind me of me back then. I got yelled at for daydreaming all the time. Mostly it was about boys."

DJ leaned her rear against the counter, snagging a carrot off the relish tray. "I wasn't thinking about boys."

"Horses?"

DJ shook her head. "About you, us, the baby." She cocked her head. "Are you *really* pregnant?"

"Either that or I have some horrific bug that attacks at odd times and makes me toss my cookies. Does it bother you, DJ?"

DJ shook her head. "I don't think so. Of course, it isn't here yet, but . . ."

"But?"

DJ struggled for words to describe her feelings without sounding like a total jerk.

"Just say it. We'll make sense of it later."

DJ stared at her mother. "That's what Gran would say."

"Oh no, I sound like my mother. After all these years of promising myself I would *never, ever* sound like my mother."

"Why not? Gran's about the coolest grown-up anywhere. She makes sense all the time."

"Not to me when I was growing up. Remember, she's *your* grandmother, and the sun rises and sets on her as far as you're concerned. And vice versa. That's the way it should be. But I grew up with her, and we had some royal battles."

"Like you and me?"

"Maybe worse." Lindy grinned and crossed from the center island, where the cook top resided, to DJ. She stroked back a strand of her daughter's hair. "All this to get around what you were going to say?"

DJ shrugged. "Maybe. I guess I get jealous sometimes." There, the words were out, and as she'd suspected, they sounded totally jerky. After all, she was almost fifteen and should be smarter than that.

"Ah, Darla Jean, you have such a gift for honesty." Lindy hugged her daughter. "My no-games girl, that's who you are. Anyone would feel jealous at times. You've been through some major stuff in the last year, and you and I were just getting our acts together when Robert and the boys stepped into the picture. Those two guys take up a lot of time and love, and I wouldn't have it any other way. But you . . ." Lindy laid her hand along her daughter's cheek. "You're the child of my heart. You came from me, and even though I forget to always tell you, I love you more every day. I never thought that would be possible. I am so proud of you I could pop, and yes, sometimes I want to smack you upside the head, as Joe would say, but I'll never stop loving you."

DJ rolled her lips together and leaned into her mother's embrace. Guess that answered *that* question, the one she hadn't even thought to ask. Was that what was behind all this? Was she afraid her mother might not love her enough? They sniffed in unison, and Lindy reached for the box of tissues.

"Adding a baby to this mix isn't going to be easy. Babies never are. But you watch, you're going to love that little one like you do the boys. And Robert promised me that God has plenty of love to go around for all of us."

"Did Robert and Gran go to the same school?" DJ could feel her smile tremble. "They say the same things."

"Them and Joe. You know how lucky we are they came into our lives?" Lindy gave DJ another hug and stepped back. "Life sure has been a roller coaster lately. You think it'll ever settle back down?"

"According to Gran, I wouldn't count on it." DJ sighed. "I'd just like to get caught up once in a while. My fingers are itching for the drawing pencils, but I've got another book report due instead. You wouldn't like to tell me about one of the books you've read?" She gave her mother a sideways, extremely hopeful glance.

"Sure I will. Which do you want? *Goodnight Moon, The Little Engine that Could*, or, I know, *Mamma, Do You Love Me?*"

"M-o-t-h-e-r! I gotta go call Amy. If she rides her bike over, can you take her home?"

"Sure. Tell her dinner's ready as soon as she gets here."

"Be thinking about a name for our card line," DJ called over her shoulder as she bounded up the stairs.

When dinner was over and the boys were parked in front of the TV with a *Veggie Tales* video, DJ, Amy, and Lindy gathered around the kitchen table. Amy spread out her latest pictures, and DJ pulled out her two latest foal drawings. The spread also included an order for more cards from DJ's Aunt Julia's friend on the East Coast and a letter from another card shop owner who'd seen their line in other stores.

"Looks to me like you two are getting more business than you can handle." Lindy smiled at one of Amy's baby pinto pictures. "This sure is a cute one."

DJ laid out another letter. "This one asks if we have any T-shirts with our pictures on them. She's sure she could sell a lot of them in her store. She's from . . ." DJ looked at the address again. "Wyoming? How'd she hear of us?"

"Word of mouth, my dear, the very best kind of advertising." Lindy flipped the pages of the ledger they'd been forced to start so they could keep track of their sales. "You have cards and frameable pictures in how many stores now?"

"Six, not including the Briones and Bottomly tack rooms," Amy replied immediately.

DJ gave her a look of awe. "How do you keep track of everything?"

"It's not like we have a million, you know." Amy held up a picture of a pinto baby looking head on into the camera. "John said I should put a striped birthday hat on this one and a message inside."

"Cool."

"You know he's in that business class? He said we should go talk with Mr. Mann about letting the class help us."

"Help us how?"

"Well, I guess they do projects, and John thought we would be a good one."

"John said *that*? Are we speaking of the same John?"

Amy punched DJ lightly on the shoulder. "Watch it, that's my brother you're talking about."

"Yeah, I know. The one who said he'd never help us again unless we paid him big bucks—and even then it was a maybe."

Lindy chuckled. "That may be, but I think he has a good idea. It looks to me like you are fast approaching the time when you will have to treat this like a real business. I know we've talked about this before, and you've done some good things like opening a business checking account and the ledger, but . . ."

"But now we need a name. And Robert said we should get business cards, too."

"I can print those from the computer, in color even. If I had a scanner, I could even print the foal pictures you draw. But when I tried the color printing, it came out shinier than what we have done at the printers."

"You might have to begin to think about bigger print runs so you can keep your costs down."

"Huh? That would cost tons more." DJ shook her head. She flipped back to the ledger. "We have a grand total of two hundred and fourteen dollars in our account."

"But you have some money still to come in, right?" Lindy checked the figures. "See here, in accounts receivable?"

"This is getting worse than algebra." DJ propped her chin up with her hands. "I'd rather draw than all this stuff."

"That's one of the problems of a business of your own. Getting all the busywork done and still having time for the creative part."

"How do you know all this stuff?"

"She got a business degree, Darla Jean Randall." Amy only used that name when she thought DJ wasn't thinking straight, or at all in some cases.

"Oh, I forgot." DJ shrugged. "So what can we call our *company*?" She giggled at the word.

"Foalin' Around?" Amy tossed into the idea pot.

"We might not want to use all foals." DJ tapped her chin with the end of her pencil. "How about DJAM. Say it as D-Jam. For our names."

"Cards by DJAM? DJAM Cards? DJAM Greetings? DJAM, Etc.? I think you need to leave it open for other products, not just cards. You already have two—cards and frameable art," Lindy suggested.

"Oh wow, frameable art. That sounds much better than pictures of foals." Amy smiled at DJ's mother. "You have good ideas."

Lindy wrote each of the suggested names on her tablet. "Why not let that percolate for a while. Seems to me you need to decide if you are going to take on any more clients."

"Sure we will." DJ and Amy nodded at each other.

"But then we have to print more stock." Amy glanced at her work sheet. "We're down to a dozen packets of foal pictures and ten of photos. Shipping these orders will clean us out."

DJ groaned. "When? Good thing the printer is open

twenty-four hours a day. We might have to be."

"It'll be easier when school is out." Lindy glanced at her watch. "We better wrap this up if you've got homework."

"So when do we talk with Mr. Mann?" Amy asked, gathering up the papers and stacking them.

"Why not tomorrow, or at least ask him about it? I could do that during study hall."

"We should go together," Amy said with a nod. "That leaves lunchtime or after school."

"Or we go in early."

"You? Early?"

"Thanks a big lot. I don't always oversleep." DJ rolled her eyes at Amy. *Great, now Mom knows I was almost late.* She waited for her mother to comment.

Amy flinched. "Sorry."

"So you need to hit the sack early, right?" Lindy said calmly.

"Uh-huh." *Whew, thought I'd had it there. Mom sure is different lately.*

"Good, then I'll take Amy home and you get on your homework. The boys can come with me." Lindy pushed back her chair. "You girls have a really good thing going here. It's going to be fun to see what all happens."

"Thanks for helping us. Oh, and I forgot, Mom said to tell you congratulations." Amy picked up her things. "You know, I like DJAM, and maybe the Etc. would be a good thing."

"Fine with me." DJ glanced at her mother, who nodded.

"So we have a company name, then—DJAM, Etc." DJ looked to her mother and Amy. "Cool, huh?"

DJ managed to stay awake through her algebra and two chapters of the book due for her report. She almost woke up when her mother turned out the light but not enough to mumble more than "Good night."

After the final bell on Tuesday, when DJ and Amy talked with Mr. Mann about their business, he invited them to speak with his class the next day. "Bring samples of all your cards and pictures, your ledger, wrapping supplies, anything you have so we can see how we can help. Mrs. Adams told me about your drawings, DJ. She's really been impressed. I'm glad you thought to come to me."

"My brother John said we should," Amy said.

"Good, glad you listened to him." Mr. Mann wrote himself a note. "I'll let your third-period teachers know so you are excused. Okay?"

The two girls high-fived each other as they raced down the concrete walks between classroom buildings. Joe would be waiting.

Once at home, DJ changed clothes and charged back down the stairs to tell her mother what had happened at the meeting, in between bites of a PB&J and glugging a glass of milk. "Where are the twins?" she finally asked.

"At our house. Mel is giving them an art lesson." Joe had come in to wait for DJ and munched a carrot in the meantime.

"You mean they're smearing paint?"

He shrugged. "Sounded like they were having fun to me. She's making lasagna tonight for us all to celebrate finishing her contract."

"We should be bringing the dinner." Lindy shook her head. "Leave it to my mother."

"That's okay. I ordered an ice-cream cake that says 'Congrats, Mel' on it."

DJ still had a hard time getting used to someone calling her grandmother Mel. She was Gran to most everyone else. Besides, Melanie was much prettier. But if Joe wanted to call his wife Mel, that was up to him.

"Let's go, kid, or your students will be there before you are." Joe heaved himself to his feet. "Thanks for the snack, Lindy. You take it easy, you hear?"

They left Lindy chuckling in the kitchen and Queenie looking sad as they went out the door.

"That dog sure took to you," Joe said as he slammed the truck door.

"I know, but she plays with the boys all the time I'm not there. I let her sleep in my room a few times, but Mom hit the roof. I think Robert would let her."

"Robert has always had dogs in the house. Your mother just needs to get used to pets."

"I've always wanted a kitten, but she said no. Wouldn't that be fun?"

"DJ, you have about as much time to housebreak a kitten as . . . well, as nothing. Thought you promised not to take on anything new?"

"I did. But I can dream, can't I?"

Joe groaned. "Sure, but your dreams have a way of coming true."

DJ shivered. She hoped the dream she'd had the night before would never come true. There'd been a fire at the barn, but she woke up before she learned if any of the horses were hurt. She rubbed the scar in the palm of her left hand and shivered again. The thought of fire made her feel like an idiot. No one else she knew went into total frozen-statue mode at the sight of flames, even birthday candle flames.

5

"OKAY, LISTEN UP. THIS IS our last class before the show."

The giggling stopped, but DJ had to admit the girls were in a wild mood. Andrew watched them as though they were some strange creatures from a distant planet. He sat on Bandit like he'd been riding for years, a picture that made DJ want to giggle herself. Andrew had come so far from the terrified little boy who used all his courage and then some just to touch the horse.

And people said kids weren't influenced by television. He'd seen someone get seriously hurt by a horse on TV and had been afraid ever since. But no longer. Or at least so it appeared today.

DJ knew how fear could leap out and attack at the oddest moments.

"Andrew, since you're the only one who seems to be listening, why don't you lead out? Circle the ring to the right at a walk."

Andrew grinned at her and gathered his reins, then nudged Bandit into a walk. The others fell in behind him, shooting DJ smiles that told her they knew what she was doing. Between the three girls and her, Andrew got all the pats he needed.

"Krissie, what's with your hands today? Angie, are you all right? Looks to me like you're having trouble breathing."

"I am, but it's getting better." The girl with long brown hair worn in a single braid coughed a couple of times.

DJ beckoned her to the center of the ring. "The rest of you keep walking."

Angie coughed again, this time what seemed like forever.

"Do you need to use your inhaler?"

"Um."

DJ took hold of the horse's reins. "Do you have it with you?"

Angie nodded as she fished in her pocket and withdrew the gray plastic inhaler. She coughed again before putting it in front of her open mouth. Letting all her air out, she depressed the button. She inhaled and tried to hold her breath, but the coughing started again.

DJ forced herself to remain calm. Last summer she'd seen Angie go into a major attack because of a beesting, and ever since then, she had a healthy respect for the terrors of asthma. "Take it easy and try again. You're doing fine, Angie, easy now." She kept her voice in the same gentle singsong she used with panicky horses.

Angie did the routine again and this time managed to hold her breath to the count of five. DJ knew because she counted in her head. "That's much better. Is it helping?"

Angie nodded. "Th-thanks." She squeezed the inhaler again, and this time her face lost the pinched look. She stuck the inhaler back in her pocket. "What am I gonna do, DJ, if something like this happens while I'm in the ring? Maybe I shouldn't try to show after all."

"You've shown before and were fine. What happened to trigger this attack?" DJ let her shoulders drop and swallowed her own fear. She felt light-headed from trying to breathe for Angie. *Thank you, God. You took care of us again. Sorry I didn't even get around to asking for help.*

"I don't know. I was fine at the barn, and then when I rode into the ring, I started coughing." Angie coughed again, but this time she could breathe deeper. "Thanks, DJ."

DJ looked up to see the other riders in a half ring around them, about ten feet away. Their faces wore the solemn look of concern. "Okay, kids, let's get back to work."

"Angie going to be okay?" Krissie asked, her blue eyes serious for a change. Her curly blond hair caught the glint of the sun.

"Sure, she's fine now. Get going." DJ just hoped Angie was as fine as she looked. And everything had been going just great. Now, how could she not worry like a mother hen when the girls went in the ring?

"That sure scared me," Samantha, the more serious of the three girls, whispered before turning away.

The rest of the class went by without incident. Her students walked, jogged, or in Andrew's case, trotted, and when the girls signaled their horses to lope, he kept on posting at the trot like DJ ordered. They all reversed and on command came to a halt in the center of the ring.

"You all need to wash your horses on Thursday and clean your tack. Samantha, looks to me like your horse needs shoeing."

"Am . . . am I going to show?" Andrew's voice trembled.

DJ shook her head. "No, this is a Western show. We have a schooling show coming up in a couple of weeks, and if you want to enter, you can then."

"We all started in schooling shows," Angie said with a smile down at the boy on the pony beside her.

"I . . . I don't have to show if I don't want to." Andrew patted Bandit's neck.

"That's right." DJ pointed them all to the gate. "See you later."

"Thanks, DJ," Angie called back.

DJ knew the girl was referring to more than the riding lesson. She followed the girls out of the ring and headed to the barn to saddle Major.

"What happened out there?" Joe asked.

"Angie had an asthma attack. Scared me spitless." Since DJ had already groomed her horse, she saddled him as she talked.

"Couldn't tell. You looked cool as a cucumber out there." Joe stripped the saddle off Ranger.

"That spitless thing is true, you know. I couldn't even swallow, but then I coulda fainted, I was trying so hard to breathe for Angie." She stopped after buckling the girth and leaned her forehead against the saddle. "Joe, I was so scared. What if she fell off her horse or passed out? She did one time."

"I know. But you handled things both times with the best of your ability and God's help." Joe hung his saddle over the aluminum bars and came into Major's stall. "We'll all just have to add Angie to our prayer lists on show days. If she feels she can do this, we sure don't want to discourage her."

"I know." DJ sucked in a deep breath and let it all out so she could relax. Shaking hands never did much for good riding, along with wobbly knees.

"Are you jumping today?"

"On Megs." She tried to chuckle, and it came out a croak. "Besides, Major and I need some flatwork anyway. Review for the dressage class tomorrow. I've skipped a couple of days, and you know what that does to our strength and suppleness."

"If it's anything like mine, you are in deep trouble." He rubbed his middle back. "I've got to watch this muscle.

When Ranger zigs, it wants to zag, so it can gripe."

"Gran gives good back rubs."

"Don't I know it." He patted DJ's shoulder. "You better now?"

She nodded and sighed again. "Being a teacher, coach, whatever you call me, is the pits sometimes. Come on, Major, we got work to do."

And work they did. She had Major trot circles, serpentines, turns on the forehand, and turns on haunches. They did them one way of the ring and then the other. By the end of the workout, they were both dripping with sweat.

Wednesday DJ woke with butterflies as bad as, if not worse than, on a show day. She and Amy had to present their business to Mr. Mann's class. And John Yamamoto was in that class. DJ ranked speaking before a bunch of kids right up there with algebra finals. Maybe she should crawl back under the covers and claim stomach flu. Her midsection felt about that bad.

"Why the long face?" Robert asked when she made it to the kitchen.

"Hi, DJ, we's going to Grandma's again. She says we paint good."

DJ looked over at the door of the refrigerator that was nearly hidden behind their paintings. "Looks good to me, too. Wish I could come." The thought sent her spiraling back through the years. Gran had taught her painting, too, and look where it had gotten her. "Gran's a great teacher. You two have fun." She patted their heads as she set her cereal bowl down on the table.

She looked up at Robert. "Amy and I are talking to the business class today."

"Uh-oh. Public speaking, the bane of human existence."

He waved a pancake turner in the air. "You want some bacon?"

DJ shook her head. "Thanks, but I don't think so."

"Funny, that's what your mother said. She's hiding under the covers. Guess we give up bacon around here for a while." He bit into a crispy slice. "Boys, here comes the bacon."

"I've got good news for everyone," Robert added. "Maria is well enough to come back to work." Maria Ramos had been the boys' nanny since their mother died. The young woman had been so sick from pneumonia that she'd been recuperating at her sister's house since the winter.

"Oh." *That means Mom will go back to work*. DJ chewed her granola and thought about that. Things sure had been nicer around here with Mom home. But Maria would do the cooking and cleaning and watch the boys until someone else came home.

"Yay, Maria's coming back." The Double Bs bounced in their chairs.

"Maria bakes good cookies." Bobby—or was it Billy—told her. If only they would make sure they sat in the same chair all the time or wore a Band-Aid, which wasn't unusual.

"Mom does, too." DJ tried to remember when her mother had baked cookies. Surely she could bake good cookies.

Getting up from the table, DJ set her bowl and spoon in the sink, then drained her glass of orange juice. "Bye, guys, have fun at school."

Queenie dogged her back upstairs, then down again to sit at the door, tail sweeping the floor. DJ bent over to pat her and got a lightning face washing in return. "Bye, dog. You be good, too. Why don't you go up and see if you can help Mom feel better." Queenie wagged her tail again and put one paw up on DJ's knee.

The horn honking reminded DJ to sling her pack on her back and use both hands to pick up the box of business things she'd collected. Since the move into the new house, she and Amy kept the extra card packets in DJ's closet.

"The anticipation is always worse than the doing," Robert called as he heard her open the door.

"Thanks for the advice . . . sorta," she called back and headed for the car.

DJ and Amy hustled their things into Mr. Mann's classroom between classes, which sent the butterflies trying new feats of fluttering.

"You do all the talking, and I'll cheer you on," DJ whispered.

"Get real." They took seats at the back of the room.

"Today we have two guests," Mr. Mann said to his class as soon as they'd settled down. "Amy Yamamoto and DJ Randall have begun a business of their own, and so far it is doing very well. They have developed and produced a line of greeting cards using drawings and photos of horses. It was suggested that they come to us and see if we might have some good advice to offer. DJ, Amy, the floor is yours."

DJ wished she could crawl out of the room on the floor that was supposedly hers.

Amy nudged her. "Come on."

They picked up their two boxes and walked to the front of the room, where they set up a display on the edge of the chalkboard and the table. Then they stood next to each other, took deep breaths, and Amy began. They took turns describing what they had done, where the cards were selling, which sold the best, and their idea for a business name. When they finished, the teacher asked if there were any questions.

When one of the students asked more about costs, Amy handed out a paper she'd prepared with that information.

"Cool," DJ whispered.

Mr. Mann took over the board and wrote down suggestions. That flew along with questions, fast and furious. No one wanted to leave when the bell rang.

"I think we should take this on as a class project," one boy from the middle aisle suggested.

"Me too" came from around the room.

"I take it that is an agreement?" Mr. Mann said, looking around the room.

When everyone nodded, he turned to the girls. "How about we set up an after-school meeting for next Wednesday? Those who can come, do so. Then we'll plan for further meetings. Is that all right with you?"

DJ started to say something, but Amy poked her and said, "That would be great. Thank you."

As the students left the room, several stopped and admired the cards. "You ought to put these in the school store," one said. "I'd buy them."

"Me too," said another. "I love horses."

John nodded to them as he and another boy walked out.

"You did very well," Mr. Mann told them as they gathered up their things. "I've never seen this group so excited about anything. We'll discuss what we can do during class and begin to lay out a proposed plan. I know of a couple of businesspeople I'd like to bring in to speak on the issues of production and marketing. If you can get away from your classes again, you are welcome to come hear them, too. But we'll make sure you get the information. I have a list of books that might be helpful for you to read, and you're welcome to use my class library of books, videos, and audio tapes."

"I think I'm about blown away," DJ admitted as she and Amy picked up their things. "I never thought about how much we needed to know."

"You've done well without a lot of experience. I'm happy to help."

"Can you believe that?" Amy said once they were alone in the hallway, her eyes wide. "That was totally awesome."

"I can't believe we're going to be late to our next class if we don't hustle."

After school, DJ climbed into the truck with her box on her lap. "Joe, you shoulda been there."

"I take it the meeting went well."

"An understatement for sure." Amy climbed in and slammed the door.

"Might hot fudge sundaes help calm you two?"

"Hot fudge sundaes are good for any time." DJ leaned her head on the seat back. "Man, I feel like I've been jumping a six-foot stone wall, without a horse."

"Are you in over your head yet?"

"Joe, it's like we're walking on the bottom of the ocean, so deep we can't even see daylight." Amy flopped like DJ.

How am I gonna do all this? DJ's mind raced. *School, classes at the Academy, shows, our business . . . sheesh.* "This all makes me tired just thinking about it."

"Me too. Maybe two hot fudge sundaes."

What is Mom going to say now?

That evening, DJ called her grandmother. "Would it be okay if I came over for a while? I really need to talk with you."

"Of course, darlin', you know you can always come here."

"I know. See you in a couple of minutes."

DJ hung up the phone, snagged her latest foal drawing from her easel, and took the stairs two at a time. "I'm going to Gran's, okay?"

"Sure, but don't be out after dark," her mother called back from the family room. "Tell Joe and Mother to come over for dessert later if they'd like."

"'Kay." DJ thought of getting her bike out but decided she could jog the short distance just as fast.

"I have our tea all ready," Gran said when DJ came through the door. "And cookies."

"Mmm, smells good in here. You've been baking?"

"She sure has." Joe picked up the tray he'd prepared. "You two want kitchen or living room? I'm going out to work in the garden," he answered in response to the questioning look DJ sent him.

"Living room." Gran hooked her arm in DJ's. "I've needed a heart-to-heart with you for some time, darlin'. I'm so glad you called."

Joe set the tray down on the footstool in front of Gran's new wing chair. "Save me some cookies, you hear?" He winked at DJ as he snagged a cookie from the plate.

"Oh, Mom said to invite you to come over for dessert later. I almost forgot."

Joe and Gran looked at each other and both shrugged. "Sure."

Gran took her place in the chair, and DJ looked up at her from her seat on the floor. While DJ had always thought her grandmother a beautiful woman, studying her beloved face in the lamplight, she realized it afresh. Gran wore love and serenity like a gossamer shawl or a second skin. Her silvering hair feathered back on the sides and waved down on one side of her forehead. DJ looked closely—sure enough, there was a dab of cerise oil paint on the side of her chin. She'd often thought Gran resembled a meadowlark, with a song of praise raised in the morning.

DJ inhaled. Fragrant cinnamon apple tea, chocolate cookies, and Gran's rosewater perfume. She always smelled fresh like the flowers she loved but without the thorns. DJ sighed and leaned against her grandmother's knee, the way she used to sit so often when they lived in their old house, before Gran married Joe.

"What's up, child?" Gran stroked DJ's hair.

DJ told her all about the business, school, and her art class. She showed her drawing and finally ran down to a close.

"Is that all?" Gran poured more tea in both their cups.

"Um, I think so. I . . . I just feel sometimes like I might snap like a rubber band that got pulled too hard, you know what I mean?"

"Sure do. And I'm not surprised you feel that way. Everyone does at times, and the pace you go . . ." Gran shook her head and chuckled. "Darlin', you make me feel like a slacker at times."

DJ traced circles on the knee of her jeans.

"That's not all, is it?"

"No." DJ turned and looked up at her grandmother, set aglow by the lamplight. She held up her left hand. "Gran, I've got to get over this fear of fire thing. It is so crazy that I freeze when I see fire." DJ looked at the small scar in the palm of her hand. "I know you're going to say we should pray about it. I *have* prayed about it—lots. But nothing seems to happen."

Gran sighed and nodded. "Sometimes it seems that way all right. Why don't the two of us pray together now, not only for the fear to go away but for wisdom in dealing with this."

DJ nodded and, with her hands clasped in Gran's,

bowed her head. Silence surrounded them—the kind of silence that is so full of peace, it makes your eyes water. DJ sniffed and leaned her head on Gran's knee.

"Father in heaven, DJ and I come to you with a special purpose tonight. We thank you for the great love you have for us and for the way you take care of us."

DJ sniffed again. *Come on, Randall, get a grip.*

"We ask that you help Darla Jean in overcoming this fear of fire. Give us wisdom to understand and the strength to carry out whatever it takes to help her through this. Father, we know we are your children and that your promises are ours. You said 'Fear not, be not afraid,' and that's what this precious girl wants, freedom from fear. We thank you that you hear us and that you will answer in your time and your way. In Jesus' precious name, amen."

"Amen. Thanks." DJ sniffed again and sighed.

Surely this would make a difference, but how soon?

6

BY FRIDAY AFTERNOON DJ figured she was caught up to about Wednesday. Maybe.

"At least I'm not showing this weekend." Major flicked his ears back and forth, listening to her, yet keeping track of everything going on around them. All the Western riders in the barns were buzzing around like yellowjackets at a picnic, washing horses, cleaning tack, last-minute clipping and grooming. "And at least the show isn't clear over in Palo Alto or something. That will be next weekend." She shivered as she thought of the big show. "How come the butterflies still get to me?"

Major shook his head and tried to nuzzle her ear when she wiped down his face.

"Better get the fly guards out, huh? They've been at your eyes."

He nosed her pockets, hoping for more treats.

"You already ate them, you big moose. My pockets are too small for as many goodies as you want."

He sighed, blowing carrot breath in her face.

"Get real. You are not abused, not one bit." She slipped the bridle in place, fastened the throat latch, then unhooked the gate and led him out of the stall. They threaded their way between all the activity and headed for the ring to warm up. Their class was due in the jumping ring, ready to go in fifteen minutes.

"DJ?"

She turned at the call from the other barn door. Angie's mother waved and headed across the graveled lot. "I just wanted to thank you for how well you handled Angie's emergency the other day. I took her into the doctor, and he put her on antibiotics—again. If we could just keep her from catching other people's germs."

"It wasn't something from here at the barns, then?"

"No, bronchitis. But we caught it right away and she feels fine again. Of course, prednisone is always a big help."

DJ breathed a sigh of relief. "It made me afraid for her to be in a show-ring, but I wasn't about to tell her that." Major nudged her between the shoulder blades.

"I fight those kinds of fears all the time, but I know that for her sake, she has to be allowed to do whatever she feels she can—like showing her horse. She sure does love that animal and being here with all of you."

"I'm glad. She's a neat kid and is becoming a good rider." Major nudged her again.

"Well, thanks again. You're her idol, you know. She wants to be like DJ." Mrs. Lincoln turned back to the barn, so DJ opened the gate and entered the ring. The warm glow went from her heart to her face and stayed there.

When Tony and Hilary joined her, they all warmed their horses up around the ring with a walk, trot, canter, and over the cavalletti. Bridget entered the ring a few minutes later and stood in the center, waiting for their attention. "All right," she said after a greeting. "Today I would like you to change horses. DJ, you take Hilary's. Tony, you on Major. And Hilary on Tony's horse. When you are ready, work your new mount around the ring a few times to become accustomed to a different horse. Do some circles and serpentines and go over the cavalletti, and then we will begin with low jumps."

DJ could feel her neck and shoulders tighten up. She dismounted and smiled at Hilary. "Got any instructions for me?"

"No, not really. Jupiter is a willing horse like Major, but he likes a firm, steady hand. He'll go for you."

DJ adjusted the stirrup leathers and mounted, settling herself not only on a strange horse but in a different saddle. She did as Bridget had ordered, feeling out Jupiter's responses and praying she wouldn't make a mistake. While she'd ridden lots of other horses, she hadn't jumped them. That was the biggest difference.

"DJ, you are behind. Use your aids," Bridget's voice cut into her concentration.

Come on, Randall, get with it. Her little voice sounded like a drill instructor in her ear.

Jupiter took the low jumps like they weren't even there. DJ counted the paces, but no matter what, he seemed to scoot out from under her. Sure she was behind, and it didn't look like she would catch up. She glanced at Major, who rocked along like clockwork.

Bridget raised the rails. Three, two, one, up and over.

Jupiter quit. He slid right into the fence, knocking the rails down with his chest and upper leg. DJ ended up on his neck, but at least she kept her stirrups and reins. She could feel her face blazing hot and knew the red could be seen for a mile or two.

Bridget came to replace the rails. "Now you see what I mean about your aids. Keep him between your hands and legs. He felt your hesitation and figured the ground was safer than the jump. You have to *ride* these other horses. You cannot be just a passenger."

DJ wanted to ride out of the ring and keep on going. Didn't she know anything about jumping? Instead, she cantered Jupiter around the ring again, settled them both, and returned to the jump. She counted the paces, kept her hands and legs firm but soft, and shifted her weight forward at just the right moment.

Jupiter sailed over the jump. With no time to cheer, she focused on the jump ahead like she knew she should and continued the round. At the finish, she felt like applauding.

Instead, Tony and Hilary did it for her.

"Not perfect, but you came together." Bridget had the others jump with their new mounts, and then the three took back their own horses.

"That was great." Tony patted Major's neck. "He is a good horse, DJ. Even when I glanced over at you, Major didn't shift; he just took the jump like a veteran."

"Thanks." DJ handed Jupiter's reins back to Hilary. "I'm sorry I made him quit like that."

"No problem. Not the first time that's happened, and it won't be the last. But you learned from it, huh?"

"Sure did. I've got a long way to go, that's for sure."

"Yeah, well, we all begin somewhere, and you really have come a long way for the short time you've been jumping. It's funny, but when things finally click for you, it's like, 'Why did I not get it sooner?' You'll get there—and soon, I bet."

"Thanks." DJ patted Major's neck and smiled up at Hilary.

"All right, now go around again on your own horse and put into practice what you learned."

DJ mounted and did as told. When would she *click*? And what was it she was missing out on?

"So your girls are all ready?" Bridget asked as DJ was about to leave the ring.

"Pretty close. They sure remind me of Amy and me back when we were beginning. Talk about gigglers. Were we that bad?"

Bridget shook her head. "You were not gigglers, but I seem to remember some wild water fights on the wash rack." Hearing shrieks from that general vicinity, they smiled at each other.

"Sometimes I feel positively old." DJ patted Major's sweaty neck.

"You always have been mature for your age. In my mind, that is one reason for your success. That and your extreme dedication."

"Extreme?" DJ kept patting Major, nearly afraid to look at her coach.

"Extreme. That is what it takes, ma petite, to go where you want to go. Watch your concentration. And watch your horse and the next jump. Always the next jump. Focus, focus, focus."

"Sheesh, that's what Robert tells me about algebra, too. You think there's a message in this somewhere?" She knew she was bordering on smart mouth, but she couldn't resist.

Bridget nodded and smiled. "Could be. See that you learn it." She gave DJ a pat on the knee, but that was nothing to the pats she'd given to her pupil's confidence.

DJ stared after her coach. Focus and quit daydreaming at the wrong times. She'd gotten in trouble for that enough this week. "Thanks, Bridget," she whispered. The rare compliments from Bridget were something to be savored, like the hot fudge sundaes with Joe and Amy. "God, I sure am a lucky kid. Thanks a ton." Her whispered prayer set Major's ears to flicking as he edged toward the barn. "Hungry, huh? Well, so am I, so let's get you cooled down and fed."

"How're things going, DJ?" Bunny Ellsindorf, one of the adult jumpers, called as she rode toward the outdoor jumping arena.

"Great. Just remind me of that tomorrow when my girls are in the ring and I'm having a nervous breakdown."

"I hear you. Joe said I could ride with you to Palo Alto next week. Is that all right?"

"Sure. I better get going. See ya."

Why'd she ask me? It's Joe's truck and trailer, after all. Maybe you didn't make her feel too welcome that last time. The little voice must have been catching some Zs; she hadn't been nagged at for a while. "I sure hope that wasn't it." She had to get better at hiding her feelings, and being polite was more important than being comfortable, according to her grandmother. After all, Bunny had been really nice to DJ in the last months, and to everyone else, now that DJ thought about it. Maybe Bunny's early weirdness had been because of moving and all that, as Joe had suggested.

DJ shook her head. Too many things to figure out—and now she could be accused of daydreaming again. Were daydreaming and trying to figure things out in the same category?

Showing was easier than coaching, on the nerves, anyway. DJ paced the side of the ring as her three students rode in, one after the other. Would Angie be all right? DJ knew that tension could bring on an asthma attack. Would Krissie's horse behave? Did any of them have even a chance of placing?

She wished she'd stayed home in bed.

"Easy, ma petite. You have done your work well with them. Now it is their turn. You must learn to relax. Otherwise you will communicate your tension to them, much like you do to a horse."

"Easier said than done," DJ muttered.

"I know." For once Bridget didn't get on her case for a comment that wasn't exactly positive. "Watching is always hard. Your two fathers nearly tore their programs in shreds when you were in the ring last week."

"They did?" DJ could feel her mouth drop.

Bridget smiled and pointed to the ring. "See how well the girls are doing. You might warn Krissie about crowding the rider ahead of her. She has a tendency to get in a hurry." Together they watched the riders circle the ring. Since it was a huge class, the chances of her three charges placing were slim.

"If Angie can keep her asthma under control, she will become a fine rider. She has a natural grace and good hands."

DJ felt as though she'd been given a compliment for herself. She'd felt the same way about Angie, and knowing Bridget agreed built her confidence in her own judgment.

"Oh no." DJ's groan made the lady in front of her turn to look. DJ shrugged at her and nibbled her bottom lip. Krissie's horse had refused to slow from a lope to a walk. And the judge had been looking right at them.

When the girls left the arena with both Angie and Samantha carrying ribbons, DJ felt like melting into the wood riser. Bridget patted her knee and rose to go check on something. DJ knew she could relax now until trail-riding. Except for Amy's classes—and there she cheered rather than stewed.

By the end of the day, the Western riders of Briones Academy had garnered ribbons of every color, including a couple of multicolored rosettes, several trophies, tack, grooming supplies, feed, and gift certificates to various horse supply places in the area. Amy and Josh looked good with a red, white, and blue rosette attached to his head-stall. While Joe didn't place, he and Ranger didn't make any obvious mistakes like in their first show, where Ranger had spooked and jumped halfway across the arena.

"Here." Amy handed DJ her camera. "It's all set, just

point and shoot. I got some real fun ones of kids and horses earlier." Amy mounted Josh and smiled at the camera. "Take two and don't move the camera this time."

"Sheesh, you want perfection or something?"

"Yes, and a good picture."

DJ braced her elbows on her chest, sucked in a breath like she'd seen Amy do, and at the moment her air was all gone, depressed the button.

"Good." Amy dismounted and led Josh over to exchange reins for camera. "Did you see Krissie's dad taking videos? I hope he got her when her horse swirled his tail and refused the walk. She needs to see what she did wrong."

"He carries his head pretty high, too. She must be keeping his reins too tight, but if she loosens them, he picks up speed." DJ turned to look at her friend. "You know what? You should be the one teaching these girls. *You're* the one who rides and shows Western, not me."

Amy put the cap on the lens of her camera. "But I don't teach and you do. You forget that? Would you rather clean stalls?"

"No." The two of them walked back to where the horses were being loaded. Mr. Yamamoto had the ramp down for the Briones six-horse trailer. With two horses already loaded, he was waiting for Amy.

"So what are you doing tomorrow?" Amy stripped her saddle off and threw the traveling sheet over her horse. Together they snapped all the buckles.

"As little as possible. Gran is having us all over to her house after church. Then I get to finish my homework, including—are you ready—a book report. Ta-da! Which I have not read, at least not more than half. So does that answer your question?"

"Uh-huh. I was hoping we could get some more packets assembled. We have the meeting after school with the business group on Wednesday." She led Josh up into the trailer, tied him, and returned. "I have some more pictures we need to think about. You gotten any new drawings done?"

DJ shook her head. "No time. I have to check on the girls, and then I'll be right back."

"They've already left," Mr. Yamamoto said. "You two get in the truck so I don't lose you again." He beckoned another horse to be led in, then they slammed the ramp shut.

The week passed in a blur. The kids at the business club meeting Wednesday were really pumped about DJ and Amy's business and asked them to make up sample packets consisting of one of each card. They planned on calling on gift and card shops to see if they could expand the local market. They also planned to call the business writer at the *Contra Costa Times*, the local newspaper, and see if she'd like to run an article on the two young entrepreneurs.

One committee would be working on a business plan for them, another on pricing for cheaper printing and assembling.

DJ and Amy rushed out of the meeting and to the Academy without time to think or talk or DJ would be late for her lesson.

When DJ arrived home, Maria had taken over the kitchen. *"Buenos dias,"* she called. "Dinner in half an hour."

"Where's Mom?"

"At the doctor's."

DJ stopped halfway up the stairs to her room and came back down to the kitchen instead. "Is she sick?"

"No, checkup. Mr. Crowder, he go with her."

"Oh. And the boys?"

"At your *abuella's* . . . er, grandmother's house. All be back soon."

Strange, DJ thought on her way up the stairs. *It's as if she's lived here all the time, but she just came back this morning.*

Saturday morning the birds were just beginning their morning muttering when DJ staggered into the bathroom. The shower on full force brought her alert. When Joe drove in, she was waiting at the door.

"Have a good day," her mother called.

"Thanks, you too." The rest of the family was going to help Andy and Sonja get DJ's old house ready to move into. They were painting the inside and working on the yard.

Joe, DJ, and Bunny crossed the San Mateo bridge with the sun just beginning to pink the western hills, but the showgrounds were in full bustle already. The line of trucks and trailers waiting to gain the parking lot extended down the block.

"So is your friend Sean going to be here today?" Joe asked.

DJ nodded. "There was a message from him on the answering machine. I had to call and apologize for mixing up the show dates. We've been playing telephone tag mostly." She turned to Bunny. "I met Sean at the drawing class I took with the artist Isabella Gant in San Francisco. He lives over here."

"With your schedule, it's a wonder anyone ever gets a chance to talk with you," Joe added.

"Less than three weeks until school is out. I can't wait."

"I can just see you sleeping in Major's stall so you won't miss time at the Academy." Bunny waved at someone who'd waved first.

"Hey, you think Mom would let me do that?" DJ gave Joe a big innocent-eyed look.

"Dream on, kid. She thinks you live there now."

When they finally pulled into the parking lot, they took the slot next to Hilary's rig.

As usual, her flat classes were an exercise in doing her best at something she was doing only because it was good for her. While it took extreme effort, she gave each event in the ring her full attention. Focus was her motto. The good thing was they were going to jump in two afternoon events. Waiting for that took patience.

Brad and Jackie arrived in time for lunch. "Sorry we couldn't be here earlier," Jackie said, handing DJ a pastrami sandwich and chips. Brad popped the top on a peach-flavored iced tea and handed it to her. "Joe says you've been doing a good job."

"I think my best. Major reminded me to just have fun and ignore the snobs. He's in such good form and having a ball. Like a little kid playing in a sandbox. He doesn't care about the other horses at all."

"Stormy says she misses you." Brad wiped his mouth with a napkin. "She said to tell you to hurry up and get up there to play with her." Stormy was the Arabian foal Brad had deeded to her after the winter foaling and flooding. He handed her a picture. "She's growing like a weed and smart as they come."

DJ wiped her fingers before taking the photo. "What a cutie. When did you take this?"

"Two days ago." Jackie glanced over DJ's shoulder. "She hardly ever stands still long enough to have her picture taken."

"You have to catch her on the run, like this one." Brad handed her another 4" × 6" photo with the filly stretched out in a gallop, her brush of a tail already upright. When it grew longer, it would flag like her mother's. "She's going to be dynamite in the ring, a natural show-off. I thought we might show her in August."

"We?" DJ slanted him a questioning look.

"Sure, you and me. By then you'll be good on halter classes. I can't wait to see the two of you out there." He handed DJ another photo. "And here's Herndon, pining away for you."

"The trainer says he is coming along great in the jumping. I can't wait for you to ride him again and tell me what you think." Jackie took a bite of her sandwich.

"He's beautiful." DJ admired the sleek, warm-blood/Thoroughbred gelding.

"He's like Major in that he thrives on competition. I've been telling Brad we should bring him down for you. We'd pay the boarding fees, of course."

DJ glanced at her watch. "I better be getting back to Major. Thanks for the lunch and the pictures. We're due in Junior Hunter class after the next one, ring two."

DJ and Major warmed up in the practice ring along with the other contestants. A breeze kept the temperature cool enough for comfort, and with the sun shining, the day seemed to have a sparkle all its own.

"Hey, DJ!" The call caught her attention, as did the wavy red hair of the young man at the ringside. DJ guided Major over to him. "Hi, Sean. I was beginning to think you weren't going to make it."

"My mom had more chores for me today than . . . well, let's just say too many." He raised his drawing pad that was tucked under one arm. "Mind if I sketch you from here?"

DJ shook her head. "Not at all, but we won't be standing to pose."

"I know. How you been?"

"Busy. Wait until I tell you about the business stuff. Mind-blowing, it is." She lifted a hand to wave a tiny good-bye. "See you later. I have two jumping classes, so wish us luck."

He nodded and anchored his pad against the post. He

was hard at the drawing before they'd gone three horse lengths.

DJ almost wished he hadn't come. Her butterflies had gone schitzo at the sound of his voice. What fun it would be to sit or stand beside him, her art pad propped up also, and work on line and value and movement of living, breathing horses and riders.

"Oh well, Major, let's just give it our best shot."

The easy course of the Hunter class raced past as they flew over the jumps. Major took them higher than necessary as if to say, "When are we going for the real stuff?" DJ didn't hurry. Jumping was jumping, and that moment of being totally airborne was what she lived for.

While they came out of the class ribbonless, DJ didn't care. So Major wasn't the prettiest horse around. *He* didn't balk like one of the warmbloods. While she tried hard not to feel the slightest glee at the other rider's consternation, DJ patted Major's shoulder to mask her smile.

Since there were only two classes between hers, she stayed in the practice ring, taking time out only for a drink that Jackie brought her. DJ introduced Sean to Brad and Jackie and left the three of them talking so she could keep Major moving.

They were number three in the jumping order.

DJ trotted Major into the ring and signaled him to canter, heading for the first jump, a simple post and rail. They cleared it with the kind of flair that kept DJ grinning. Straight ahead, she focused on the center of the oxer and counted the paces to herself. They lifted off at the precise moment and soared over the jump, landing with perfect timing, eyes on the next.

The triple with the highest bar in the center came after a curve in the corner of the ring. "Easy, fella, let's not rush it. Two, three, four, and . . ." They lifted again, clearing the three bars like they were one.

It sounded like a pop as Major's front feet hit the ground. Instead of striding forward, he crashed to the ground. DJ flew straight over his head.

7

DJ HIT THE GROUND WITH HER SHOULDER and rolled.

"Major!" Dust filled her mouth and her eyes. Who was screaming? She lay still only for a moment, fighting to get the air back in her lungs. *Major! Is he down? Oh, God, no. Please don't let him have a broken leg. Please.* Thoughts flew like the dust that rose in a cloud around her.

She wriggled her hands and feet and paused to attempt another breath. She coughed on the intake of dust. Sure that all was in working order, she moved to a sitting position. "Major."

"DJ, are you all right?" Brad and Bridget reached her at the same time.

"Don't move." Joe cracked the order as if he were still back on the police force.

"Where's Major?" DJ rubbed the dirt from her watering eyes and tried to get up. Hands on both sides held her down.

"I'm fine! Where's Major?"

"Right behind us," Joe's voice rang in her ear, his hands gentle on her neck. "Can you move your fingers? Toes?"

"Joe, I did all that. What are you not telling me?"

She could hear people talking around them, but the silence from the stands sent shivers up her spine. She gritted her teeth. "Let me up! I just got the breath knocked out of me."

With hands assisting her on both sides, she got to her feet. Applause broke out. She turned to see Major dripping sweat, holding one front foot off the ground. Bridget was examining his leg, running soothing fingers down the flat bones.

"It is not broken," she said, glancing up at DJ. "I think it is in his shoulder."

"That's the one that's had problems before." DJ fought back the tears. "I heard a pop or crack when we landed."

Shudders wracked her horse. "He's in terrible pain."

"Or shock." Bridget stood up and turned to the ring manager. "We must get him out of here."

Dr. Jones, the veterinarian for the show, jogged across the arena. "What've we got?" He stroked Major's neck and down his leg, then went back to the shoulder. "Up here, huh?" With gentle fingers he probed the injured area. "We better get him X-rayed right away. I called for my trailer." He pointed beyond the entry gate. "It'll be right there in a couple of minutes. You want to lead him, or shall I?"

"I will." DJ sniffed back the tears threatening to drown her eyes. She rubbed Major's ears and down his cheek. "Okay, fella, let's get out of here."

"Here." Brad took the horse blanket Jackie handed him and laid it over Major's back. "We'll get the tack off in the trailer."

DJ took two steps toward the gate, and Major lurched on three legs beside her. Joe walked on his other side, keeping one hand on the horse's soaking wet neck. Applause broke out in the bleachers as they limped out of the arena.

The tears snuck under her control and rolled down her cheeks, but DJ ignored them completely as she murmured a love song to her injured friend. Her *Oh, God, please help us* kept a staggering pace with them.

They stopped outside the gate to give Major a rest, then made their ponderous way up the ramp and into the trailer. Brad stripped off the tack so DJ and Joe could buckle the blanket around the shaking horse.

Both DJ and Joe kept up their running comfort sounds as they took care of the horse they both loved. *If there's a break in the shoulder, they'll say to put him down. God, please, please, I can't lose Major this way. It's all my fault. I . . . oh, God, please, please.*

"Okay, let's give him a shot of this to help with the pain. As soon as we get to the clinic, we'll give him a tranquilizer, too. That'll help more than anything." Major never even reacted to the injection.

DJ and Joe both rode in the trailer with her horse as the truck pulled them slowly out of the grounds.

"Easy, old man," Joe murmured, stroking the horse's neck. "You're going to be all right."

"I shouldn't have tried jumping him anymore. Oh, Major, I'm so sorry." Even with the blanket over him, Major continued to shiver and drip sweat. "Joe, he hurts so bad. Look at him."

"I know. But he's tough. He's been through a lot and come back. Don't go giving up on him yet. Besides, a lot of this is most likely shock, too."

"Giving up! I just want him to not hurt so. Can't they give him something more?"

Major shifted his weight and grunted.

"We'll get a sling under him and take the pressure off. That should ease it considerably."

Several hours later, Dr. Jones delivered the terrible news.

"I wouldn't count on ever showing him again, let alone jumping. We'll have to see how lame he is after the shoulder heals."

"How long will that take?" DJ asked, afraid of the answer.

"Best case scenario, several months. Worst case, you might have to turn him out to pasture and let him live out his life in peace."

DJ studied the vet. He didn't know the heart of this horse, only the injury. And he hadn't said to put him down. *Thank you, God, for that.* "But he'll be able to walk again?"

"Oh yes. The muscles are badly torn, and there could be a stress fracture. But we won't know that until it starts to heal. If he were a million-dollar horse, we could do surgery and stitch the ligaments together, but he's not worth putting that kind of money into."

DJ felt like smacking the man. How would he know the worth of her horse? But she had to admit he was right. She didn't have the thousands of dollars needed for a surgery like that. And why put Major through so much anyway? "Just make him quit hurting so bad."

"I've given him more Bute and another tranquilizer. Once he's able to put some weight on that foot, you can come take him home. Riding that far in the trailer would be terribly hard on him now."

Major turned away at the horse cookie DJ offered him and just leaned his head against her shoulder. It was all she could do to walk away from him, but with Joe on one side and Brad on the other, she didn't have much choice.

"We's sorry for Major," Bobby said when DJ got home. Brad had called ahead and told them all what had happened.

"We been praying for him." Billy, who sported a Band-Aid on the right side of his forehead, added. He'd tipped off his bike and skinned himself up, so now it was easy to tell them apart.

"Thanks, guys." DJ dropped to her knees and hugged them close, an arm around each. She fought back the tears again. "Major's going to be all right. He just needs lots of time."

"When can he come home?"

"Not sure yet."

Brad and Jackie stood right behind her. "We could take him up to our place, where we have the equipment to care for him, then let him out to pasture as soon as he can handle it."

DJ shook her head. "Then I can't see him. I'll take care of him."

Robert shook his head. "I should have gotten going on the barn here when I wanted to. Then he could be right out our back door."

"Coffee's ready, and I made some sandwiches," Lindy called from the kitchen.

"Come on, folks, let's eat." Robert led the way, and they all gathered around the table.

As they sat down, all DJ could think of was Major at the clinic, a sling holding him high enough so only the tips of his hooves touched the floor. He was such a trooper, he hadn't even fought the restrictions, as if he understood every word DJ said to him, telling him that it was all for his own good. But when she'd wanted to stay there, she met a wall of resistance from all the adults around her.

"You let us take care of him for a couple of days, and then you'll have plenty to do." While the vet made all kinds of sense, DJ felt like screaming. Instead, she'd hugged Major one more time and was escorted out to Brad's car. Joe had

gone back to the showgrounds to load up Bunny's horse and trailer him home.

"Darla Jean, you need to eat and then hit the sack."

Her mother laid a hand on DJ's shoulder. She flinched in pain.

"Has anyone looked at this?"

DJ shook her head. "It's just tender, that's all. I'm going to soak in the Jacuzzi before I go to bed."

"Some liniment might help you, too." Brad's brow furrowed with concern.

DJ nodded. All of a sudden her eyes felt so heavy they pulled her head down. All she could think of was bed. She blinked a couple of times.

"Do you need X rays?" Lindy probed the sore shoulder gently.

"M-o-m. That's not the worst fall I've taken. I'm fine." She tried to keep the irritation out of her voice, but from the look on Robert's face, she knew she hadn't succeeded. "Sorry."

"DJ, we need to be going pretty soon," Brad said a few minutes later. "But I want to say something first."

DJ dragged her mind back from Major's suffering. "What?" She rolled her shoulders to see if she could ease the ache there, too. Inside and out she was one big ball of hurt, but she wasn't about to admit it. Her pain was nothing compared to Major's. If only she'd listened to Brad earlier and jumped Herndon, then Major wouldn't be suffering like he was.

"Jackie and I would like to bring Herndon down for you tomorrow." He thought a moment. "No, it will have to be sometime Monday. I talked with Bridget, and she has another stall available. That will give you the week to work with him, and then you can decide if you are ready to enter him in the show next weekend."

"He's been doing well for the trainer. I'd hoped you

could work with John on Herndon before you took him in the ring, but with this . . ." Jackie raised her hands and dropped them.

DJ looked from one to the other and then to Robert. "I . . . I . . ." Tears stung the backs of her eyes and she sniffed them away. *N-o-o-o. I want Major. Major is my horse.*

"Unless you'd rather not. I . . . I just thought . . . well, Jackie and I can't think of any other way right now that we can help you get your dream."

"Please, DJ." Jackie leaned forward. "Please let us help."

DJ looked from Robert to her mother and back at Brad and Jackie. "This . . . this is all happening so fast. I thought Major and me . . . I mean . . ." She closed her eyes and slumped against the chair. "I guess I really don't have any choice, do I?"

"You always have a choice, Darla Jean, remember that." Brad used her full name.

Her eyes fluttered open. "Then . . . then I choose to ride Herndon." She sat up straight again. "Thank you for loaning him to me. I'll do my best to take care of him." *Hope you do better taking care of Herndon than you did Major*, the little voice in her ear buzzed like a pesky mosquito.

Jackie shook her head. "Herndon is not on loan, DJ. He's yours."

DJ stared at her, her chin flopping on her chest.

Herndon! Herndon was hers? Her heart felt as though it would thump its way clear of her chest and run off by itself.

8

"HELLO, THIS IS DJ RANDALL," DJ said into the phone Monday morning. "Could you tell me how my horse Major is?"

"He's doing as well as can be expected. He ate, he's drinking, not fighting the sling. We'll most likely lower him a bit so he can put his other three feet on the ground, but still keep the sling on so he can rest in it. . . ." The vet paused. "You can come and get him in a few days, I'm sure. As soon as he can put weight on that foot."

"Thank you." DJ laid the phone back in the cradle before the tears could reach her throat. *You will not cry.* She picked up her backpack and headed down the stairs. When she had suggested she should be at the Academy when Brad brought Herndon if he came during school hours, the look on her mother's face said otherwise. DJ had known it was a useless suggestion, but it never hurt to ask. Besides, she wanted to save her ammunition for when Major got home. She *had* to be at the barn to care for him. After all, he'd injured himself jumping at her command.

"How is he?" Robert asked when she entered the kitchen. Maria motioned toward the table and set a plate of scrambled eggs with ham in front of DJ.

"The vet said he's doing about as well as can be expected." DJ looked up at their nanny, cook, and house-keeper. "Thanks, Maria. Hope I have time to eat all this. You want to make me fat?"

"You need more." Maria motioned around her body.

"You mean I need more . . ." DJ's palms curved around her upper body. "See, flat as a board."

Maria shook her head, her dark hair swinging in the motion. "No, no, not what I say." Her brown eyes sparkled. "You eat." She pointed at the plate and turned back to the stove.

"You better get used to this," Robert stage-whispered from around the paper he'd been reading. "She is a tyrant about eating right."

"You say right, Mr. Robert. I cook, you eat."

"How's Mom?"

"Morning miseries. I'm going to get her some Sea Bands this morning. One of the girls in the office swears by them. Lindy wants to go back to work, but I don't see how, as miserable as she is."

"What are C bands?"

"They're elastic bands with a button that presses on a nerve center to stop motion sickness. Someone developed them to keep people from being seasick."

"Oh. Is being pregnant always like this?"

"I don't think so. Some women get morning sickness worse than others."

A car honking made DJ shovel the last of the eggs in her mouth and drain her glass of milk. "Thanks, Maria. See you, Robert. Give the boys a hug for me." She winced as she hobbled out the door with Queenie right beside her. Sore everywhere didn't even begin to cover it. "Stay." DJ pointed at the steps, and the dog sat down, her pink tongue lolling out the side of her mouth. Her ears stood straight up, and the whine carried to the car.

"Boy, do you have a good dog there," Amy said as DJ

climbed in the backseat with her.

"I know, she understands everything I say. I told her to stay only once, and she sat just like that. Her other family trained her well." She slammed the car door behind her. "Hi, Mrs. Yamamoto."

"How's Major?" The driver glanced in the rearview mirror as she jockeyed the car around the central turnaround. Newly planted shrubs filled in the spaces between rocks and a couple of flowering cherry trees.

DJ filled them in on what had happened since the show. Each time she told the story she could feel the tears burn behind her eyes, but she kept them at bay.

"Isn't it weird that now you're going to ride Herndon whether you wanted to yet or not?"

"I know. But I sure wish it hadn't been at Major's expense. I shoulda . . ." When DJ closed her eyes, she could hear the pop and felt airborne all over again. She could see Major with one foot off the ground and dripping with sweat. As Gran had reminded her on the phone, she had much to be thankful for. Major could have broken a leg and have to be put down. He was still her friend whether she ever rode him again or not.

"Darla Jean Randall, you know better than to talk like that. You can't keep reliving the past." Mrs. Yamamoto shook her head as she talked.

DJ looked at Amy and shrugged. "You two sure sound alike. I know. But . . ."

"No buts." Amy crossed her arms. "If you really want to jump in the Olympics, you have to keep moving forward."

"Now you sound like Bridget and Gran all rolled into one."

Amy grinned and nodded. "Who do you think I listen to?"

"So do I, you know that."

"Yep, and I'm going to make sure you think positive all

the time. Gran, Joe, and I made a pact."

"You did what?"

Mrs. Yamamoto stopped the car by the school curb. "You two have a good day. Remember, Amy, I'll be picking you up half an hour early for your orthodontist appointment."

Amy rolled her eyes. "I know. You want to make my mouth hurt again."

"What's that about positive talk?" DJ nudged her friend as they clambered from the car and slung their packs over their shoulders. They waved good-bye and headed for their lockers.

Herndon hadn't arrived by the time DJ raced into the barn. She checked his stall to make sure there was bedding in it, filled the water bucket, and put a leaf of hay in the corner manger. She stayed away from Major's stall, wishing she'd taken time to call the veterinarian again.

She was on her way to check the duty board when Brad's truck and trailer rig turned into the Academy. She pointed to the area off to the side where they usually unloaded horses and stopped by the truck door.

"Hi, Deej. You ready for him?" Brad had the window rolled down and rested his arm on the doorframe.

"Sure enough." She pointed to her pockets. "Even came prepared with horse cookies."

"He'll love you forever." Jackie opened her door and got out. "Let's get him out of the trailer. You have a lesson pretty soon, right?"

"Right."

"I wanted John to come down and work with you on Herndon, but he wasn't available. It's been a while since you rode him."

"Too long a while."

Brad unhooked the tailgate, and he and DJ lowered it to the ground. "But I know Bridget will size him up immediately. Just remember, DJ, that he's a lot more highstrung than Major and not as push-button. You'll need to really ride him, where Major would just take you over the fences."

"But this big guy loves to jump, and once the two of you learn to really work together, he should take you far." Jackie talked over her shoulder as she entered the trailer to back the big gelding out. Herndon exited the trailer as if he were a prince or maybe a king surveying his realm. Head high, ears pricked, he stood at attention. Jackie let him look around, and only when he blew and sighed did she tug on his lead shank and walk forward.

DJ led the way to his stall, where they removed the traveling sheet and let him sniff his surroundings. After he checked things out, he came to DJ, who stood in the corner, waiting. She held out a horse cookie on her flat palm and he nibbled it up, barely touching her skin. Before he'd finished that one, he nosed her hand and up her arm. He sniffed her hair, her face, and back to her hand. When he sighed again, she gave him another cookie.

"Let's lunge him a bit to get the kinks out." Jackie snapped a lead shank back on Herndon's halter. Once outside, the tall gelding trotted around at the end of the line, checking out his surroundings and giving a kick once in a while for good measure. He tossed his head and danced to the side when Jackie began drawing in the line and looping it in her other hand. "That should help, but as you can tell, he's pretty frisky." She handed DJ the lead shank. "Go for it; he's all yours."

DJ swallowed and took in a deep breath. "I can never thank you enough."

"You don't need to. Just do your best with him, and we'll

be right behind you all the way." Jackie gave DJ a smile that made her eyes burn.

"Okay, big fella, let's get you tacked up and out in the ring so you can see the rest of your new world." DJ and Jackie worked together giving him a quick brushing, then setting pad and saddle in place and pulling the girth tight.

"He has a tendency to suck in a breath when you tighten this, so wait and tighten it again in the ring. He's a bit of a snob, you know, but once he decides he's your friend, it's for life." Jackie stroked Herndon's face and rubbed his ears. "He loves molasses on his feed, that's a real treat. He only tolerates the horse shoer. We had him shod just last week, so he'll be fine until later in July."

"They'll do fine, mother hen." Brad unhooked the stall door. "Let's go."

DJ led her new horse out to the covered arena at the front of the barn. Even walking him felt different from walking Major. Herndon's stride was longer, and he didn't keep his nose right near her elbow as Major did.

"You need to watch him," Jackie said. "He has a tendency to step on your feet, as if his own weren't enough."

"Thanks, I'll remember that."

Brad swung the gate open, and DJ led Herndon inside. With Jackie holding the reins, she tightened the girth, checked the bridle, and gathered her reins, then mounted in one graceful motion. While Major wasn't small at fifteen and a half hands, with Herndon's additional four inches, DJ felt like she could see over the barn. She patted her horse's neck, leaned slightly forward, and with a nod to Brad and Jackie, signaled Herndon to walk.

Herndon even walked differently. "Guess I knew all this when I rode you before, but now that you're mine, it seems more important." His ears flicked back and forth, listening to her and checking out everything around him. She walked him once around, then squeezed her calves for a trot. She posted easily as his trot lightly bounced her out of the saddle. She trotted him in figure eights, circles, serpentines, and across the diagonal.

As he warmed up, she began working on the dressage techniques she'd done with him in the spring. She practiced haunches in, shoulder in, and cantered, everything in both directions of the ring.

Brad signaled her over. "So how does he feel?"

"Good . . . responsive." DJ patted the horse's neck and smoothed his mane to the side. "You want to come with us to the jumping arena?"

"Of course." Brad swung open the gate, and DJ rode Herndon through. Other riders continued around the arena; some waved to DJ, congratulating her on her new horse, asking her how Major was doing. The speed with which news passed around the Academy always amazed DJ, but now she could feel a warm surge in her heart region. They all cared about her and Major. What a gift to have so many friends. She promised herself to tell Gran about it. After all, Gran said blanket prayers were good, too, and that she prayed for all those at the Academy as part of her regular prayer list.

A quick twinge of guilt followed the comfort. DJ couldn't say that *she* prayed regularly for all of them like that, more only when there was a real problem. Not that she hadn't prayed for Major. He'd been on her mind every other minute all night and day.

Brad and Jackie walked beside her out to the sandy jumping arena.

"You know, Deej, you are one lucky kid."

"I know, but what makes you say that now?"

"To be starting out in a place like this. Not only is Bridget a great trainer and coach, but the people here are pretty special, too. I watch how you all cheer one another on. And the feeling here . . ."

"What he's trying to say, DJ, is that many places aren't like this at all. Some places the competition is incredibly fierce and the back-biting, ugh. You've got to be aware, though, that as you travel to other shows, that nasty stuff goes on. We just don't want it to backwash onto you." Jackie stuck her hand through the crook of Brad's arm. "The horse show world can ruin people of lesser moral character or tender sensibilities. You have to be real strong."

They stopped at the gate, and Brad opened it for her. "Why don't you do the cavalletti at first? I've set them for his stride."

DJ nodded. She'd already planned on that. She rotated her shoulder. It ached and felt tight. Likewise her hip. Signaling Herndon around the ring, they came up to the rails laid parallel on the ground. After walking him over them twice, she increased the pace to a slow trot.

Herndon snorted and shook his head, pulling against the bit. DJ kept a firm hand on the reins.

"You just behave yourself. I don't care if you don't like this slow stuff. We're going to do this until I say we jump. Or rather until Bridget does."

He pulled again, trying to jig. DJ kept him going straight, using her legs to push his hindquarters straight. While he did manage a jig step every once in a while, he responded to her aids. He twitched his tail, and she could feel his hindquarters gather for a buck.

"No, you don't!" She tightened the reins and brought him to a standstill. "Now, Herndon, get this through your head. I am the boss, and I say what we do and don't do. You hear me?"

His flicking ears said he did, and she signaled him into a canter around the perimeter of the jumps, cutting a diagonal and turning the other way. When she could feel him relax again, she slowed and let him blow, then signaled him forward.

DJ looked up when she had Herndon going forward in a relaxed walk. Bridget had joined Brad and Jackie at the fence. Joe was crossing the gravel to watch with them, too. "Great, all we need is an audience. You get on your best behavior and stay there." She made her voice firm.

Herndon reminded her a bit of Patches, the horse she'd trained for Mrs. Johnson. He would take advantage of any slip on her part. *Concentrate. Focus.* The words hammered in her head.

"All right, DJ, pick up a trot, circle, and pop over the low jump in the middle of the ring." Bridget and Brad entered the arena and began moving standards and bars around.

DJ ignored them and let Herndon speed up his trot. He nicked two of the cavalletti bars and popped over the jump. *Big mistake. You shouldn't have let him quicken like that. Come on, get with it.*

"Okay, goof off, let's do that again and behave yourself this time." DJ counted the paces from the cavalletti to the jump, making sure her horse kept an even pace, much slower than he liked. His ears showed his disgust as plainly as if he'd said the words.

DJ wanted to laugh at him. But she was fast realizing that he needed a firm and consistent hand. She took him around twice more and could feel him settle down to work.

"All right," Bridget called from the center of the ring, "follow the pattern we have set and make sure his pacing is consistent. We are not in a hurry here. If he breaks into a slow canter, let him go. Otherwise, bring him back to a trot if he rushes."

"Okay." Inside DJ wanted to take the higher jumps as badly as Herndon did, but she knew better.

Around they continued with Bridget calling advice

when needed. DJ could feel moisture trickling down her back, and Herndon's shoulders wore sweat patches like dark paint. The longer they worked, the more he settled down, no longer fighting her restraints.

Bridget raised the bars a notch, and they continued with the same pattern. Now they had a spread that included both single and double jumps, with the higher rails to the back.

"Look toward the next jump. He is going to go where you are looking."

DJ nodded. She'd glanced up when she heard a shout from the barn. Around again. She knew they hadn't done a perfect round yet. Little things like getting left behind, just like she had with Hilary's horse. Herndon used himself so much more than Major ever did.

Bridget raised the bars another notch.

At the in and out Herndon quit.

9

"OOF!" *YOU JERK!* DJ wasn't sure if she meant the horse or herself.

She pried herself off the horse's neck and spit out a bit of mane hair. Settling back in the saddle and finding her right stirrup took a couple more triple-time heartbeats. She straightened her helmet, collected her reins, and sucked in a deep breath. She and Herndon let out their breath at the same time.

"Okay, fella, let's go back to the beginning. Sorry I dropped you. It won't happen again, but you could be a little more forgiving, you know."

Herndon snorted as DJ turned him and ordered a trot for them both to get their equilibrium back. *Oh, Major, I miss you so. God, I know you know what's best and are taking care of all of us. Keep me on this horse, please, and help us learn to work together. Feels to me like I'm getting worse, not better, at this.*

She squeezed him into a canter and focused on the jump in front of them. One at a time, count, pay attention, focus. *Three, two, one, and up. Nice and easy. Three, two, one, and up.* She felt him hesitate out of the in and out but drove him straight forward and they cleared it without a hitch. He twitched his tail when he landed as if to say, "See, it wasn't my fault."

"Again," Bridget called when DJ finished the round.

"You know, if you'd settle down, you wouldn't work up such a sweat." She still wasn't sure if she was talking to the horse or herself.

Her legs felt like rubber when she finally finished. This was harder than the show-ring any day.

"Not bad for working with a new horse." Bridget stroked Herndon's neck. "You have to watch him, though, and yourself. He will not tolerate some of the things you get away with on Major."

"I'm beginning to understand what a neat horse Major is. Herndon doesn't seem to be sneaky like Patches, though."

"No, but he wants to make sure you know what you are doing. Trust will come with time, for both of you." Bridget turned to Brad and Jackie. "DJ is very fortunate to have someone like you in her life at this point. Losing Major without another mount would have been disastrous to her career."

"Oh, I have a feeling that between Robert and her grandparents, there would have been another horse rather soon." Joe nodded as he spoke. "But most likely not quite the quality we have here." He looked up at DJ. "You look mighty fine on him, kid." He winked at her. "Even up on his neck, although I wouldn't go so far as to say that looked either graceful or comfortable."

DJ grinned down at him. "Yeah, well, I've seen you in some rather laughable poses with Ranger. One day I thought maybe you were trying to bulldog him."

"Can you beat that?" He turned to Bridget. "No respect, I get no respect around here."

That brought a laugh from all of them, and DJ dismounted. It felt like a mile farther down than from Major's back. How long would it be before she quit comparing the two horses?

"With Herndon, you could enter dressage shows, too, if you want." Bridget smiled at DJ.

DJ groaned. "I can't keep up with what I have now."

"I know. I just thought I would make the suggestion."

"You're kidding, right?" DJ felt her stomach plummet. What if Bridget really thought that was what was best for her? *I don't want to show dressage. I want to jump.* But she caught the twinkle in Bridget's eyes and breathed a sigh of relief.

"You had her going there." Joe threw an arm over DJ's shoulders. "Come on, let's get him cooled down and used to his new stall. Maybe you should stay with him tonight so he doesn't feel lonesome."

"J-o-e."

"How about I call your mom and ask her if we can take everyone out for pizza?" Brad walked on Herndon's other side.

"Fine with me. I've got lots of homework, though, so it can't be late."

"Should we order it in?"

"Whatever." DJ led Herndon back in his stall and swapped his bridle for a halter. Herndon stepped forward to snag a wisp of hay and planted his hoof right on top of DJ's foot.

"Ow!" DJ smacked his shoulder at the same time as he shifted away. "You big . . . big . . ."

"Horse?" Joe arched an eyebrow.

Pain radiated up her leg. She felt like kicking him with her other foot, but then what would she stand on?

"Sorry, DJ, are you all right?" Jackie asked.

"I will be." DJ glared at the gelding eyeing her with a puzzled look. "You know what you did, so don't try to blame it on me!" Her voice snapped where her hand wished to slap. "And you can bet I'll be more careful around you, too." She wished she could rub her foot, but instead she finished removing her tack. Brad took the saddle from her to keep her from limping up to the tack room. Joe snapped on the lead shank and led Herndon out of the stall.

"You go put your foot up for a minute. That'll make it feel better. And some ice wouldn't hurt." He led the big horse off to the grassy area by the hot walker, where countless cooling horses had worn a groove around the green.

"I'll call your mother," Brad called back from up the aisle.

"Are you all right?" Jackie asked again.

"It's not the first time this has happened, and I'm sure it won't be the last."

"Not unless you stay totally away from horses and barns and shows and such."

"When pigs fly."

"I know, me too."

DJ sat down on a straw bale by the tack room, kept there for saddle-soaping parties. She propped her foot up and leaned against the wall.

"You all right, DJ?" The concern showed on Bunny's face as she came around the corner.

"Mashed foot." DJ positioned the ice bag over her toes.

"That new horse of yours is gorgeous."

"Thanks. I have a lot to learn on him."

"One thing, keep your feet out from under his, huh?"

DJ nodded. "See ya." She waved as Bunny headed out the door. How strange it seemed to be sitting down and not rushing all over the place.

"We're bringing the pizza," Brad announced. "How about we go get that and you come with Joe. I called Gran, too."

"Okay."

"What kind do you like? Besides the supreme with everything, that is."

"Canadian bacon with pineapple, extra cheese, thick crust."

"Any other favorites?"

"Mom always says no anchovies."

"Got it."

By the time they'd all eaten their fill of pizza, were entertained by the twins, admired Gran's latest book, and talked about the barn Robert had laid out—along with a corral and pasture in their backyard—DJ wished she could blow off her studies and continue relaxing. After all, how often did a girl have such a wide family all together in one place and having a good time? At least not too many she'd heard of. Other kids had family horror stories to stand one's hair on end.

But there hadn't been an algebra quiz today, which meant Tuesday was a strong possibility. "Sorry, but can I be excused? I've got to hit the books."

Robert nodded and smiled at her. "I'll send them up to say good-bye when the party breaks up."

Before she opened her school books, DJ called the veterinary hospital again to check on Major. The night assistant said he was a sweetheart and so good when they had to move him. He was alert, eating, and resting the tip of his hoof on the rubber mat. They kept the sling just tight enough to give him extra support when he tired.

"Thanks. Give him a hug for me, will you? And he loves both carrots and horse cookies."

"I know that, hon. He checks out everyone's pockets. You quit worrying about him, you hear. He'll be home soon."

After hanging up the phone, DJ attacked her algebra with a vengeance. If Major could handle an injury like that with such grace, she could handle algebra. She had most of the problems finished, with only a question or two for her math coach, Robert, when Brad and Jackie knocked on her half-open door.

"Come in." DJ pushed her books aside.

"We need to be going." Brad handed her an envelope. "This is information on a week- or two-week-long jumping school back in New Jersey put on by a couple of USET members near the headquarters. I'd like to see you go."

"Really?" DJ folded open the sheets of paper. "Wow." She looked up at her father. "Has Mom seen this?"

"M-hm. I gave her a copy. Just think about it, okay? Other kids go to sports camps all the time."

"It would be a really great experience," Jackie added.

"But . . . but . . . I can't afford something like this." She pointed to the cost of the camp at the bottom of the page. "And it says I would have to bring my own horse, too. I don't think so. Mom will never let me go." She shook her head the entire time, whether from shock or resistance she wasn't sure which. *Oh, but what I would give to do something like this.*

10

"TAKE OUT PENCIL AND PAPER, PLEASE."

The class groaned in unison. Mr. Henderson waved his list of problems, gave an evil laugh and matching grin, then turned to begin writing the algebra problems on the board. Along with all the other kids, DJ took paper from her binder and began writing. The only thing missing was the dread that used to make her freeze, unable to think through what little she did know. Now, thanks to Robert's coaching, everyone in the family praying for her, and real practice in concentration plus a positive mind-set, algebra was only hard, not impossible.

The first problem was one she and Robert had reviewed the night before after everyone else went home. She whipped through that one. By the time the teacher asked them to exchange papers, she'd even started on the extra-point problem.

She missed one. The day she got a perfect paper, she knew she'd faint. Right out there on the floor, flat out. But flunking was a thing of the past, and that alone set her singing her way through the rest of the day. That along with another good report on Major.

"Mom!" DJ called as soon as she got in the door after school.

"She gone back to work." Maria shut off the vacuum cleaner in the living room. "What you need?"

"Fiddle. I was hoping she would take me over to see Major."

"Bad traffic time."

"I know, but sheesh, I want to see him so bad."

"You ask Joe?"

"He can't. He's got a lesson this afternoon." DJ sighed. "I've got the beginning riders, too, but I was hoping." She started up the stairs to her room. "Where are the boys?"

"Taking a nap."

"Sick?"

"No. Time out."

DJ nodded and rolled her lips to contain her grin. The look on Maria's face said it all. The twins had pushed the nanny's buttons one too many times. They could be obnoxious when they tried, sometimes without even trying.

"Where's Queenie?"

"She time out outside."

DJ glanced from Maria toward the French doors that led to the deck beyond the family room. She started to ask if Queenie could come in, then thought the better of it. Instead, she headed for her room to change into barn clothes.

When she came back down, she turned into the kitchen. Snagging an apple from the bowl on the counter top, she opened the refrigerator and grabbed a juice box and the block of cheese. After cutting herself a chunk, she put it back. The note on the refrigerator door said Robert would be home late.

"See ya. I'll be home around six." She waved to the woman now dusting the new furniture and went to get her bike. Since Joe was already working with his trainer, she'd ride over to the Academy. By the time she got there, she was breaking a sweat. Even for late May, it was hot out.

While Herndon had his head hanging out the door, he didn't nicker when he saw her. One more way to miss Major. He took the carrot she offered and crunched that, his large, dark eyes seeming to study her as if to figure out why he was in this strange barn with this strange person. When she offered him another carrot, he took that, too, but without the nuzzling of Major—more like treats were his due.

"They shoulda named you Prince or King or something. I think you're a snob."

He backed up when she entered the stall and snapped a lead chain on his halter and over his nose, just in case. Every other time she'd worked with him, Brad or Jackie had been near. She wasn't taking any chances. But he walked beside her out to the hot walker, only nicking the back of her boots with one hoof.

"I've got to watch you every minute, don't I?" She snapped the lead shank from the circular machine onto his halter and stepped back. The creaking song of the hot walker in motion followed her back to the barn.

By the time she had his stall cleaned, new bedding spread, and clean water and fresh hay in their respective places, it was time to go check on her students.

"Hey, Ang, how ya feeling?"

"Fine." Angie turned from grooming her horse. "Herndon is a hunk, for sure."

"Thanks. He thinks so, too." DJ studied the girl and her horse. "You know, if you dampened your brushes, you could cut down on the dust when you're grooming. That might help the breathing." *Why didn't I think of that before?* DJ shook her head. Sometimes . . .

She cruised by Bandit's stall to find Andrew talking to his horse like they'd been friends forever. DJ curbed the desire to give the slender little boy a hug. She was so proud of the way he worked to overcome his fear of horses she could burst.

Now, if only they could find a pony like Bandit for the twins. Or two of them, as Robert had suggested.

By the time the class was finished, the giggling girls had transmitted their disease to DJ and even Andrew, who usually looked at life through serious glasses. She swung open the gate to let them ride out and shook her head.

That sent them into peals of laughter as they rode back to the barn.

"Who put a quarter into their giggle boxes?" Bunny asked as she led her horse up to the gate.

"Got me. But it's contagious, so watch out. Did you see? Even Andrew was almost laughing."

"I saw." Bunny nodded. "You've done so much for that little boy, DJ. I hope you realize what a gift you've given him."

"I just helped him along. He gave himself the gift. He overcame that fear by plain old guts." DJ watched the boy dismount and lead his horse into the barn. The scar itched in the palm of her hand. What had she done to overcome her fear of fire? *Nothing, that's what.*

She hoped her thoughts weren't showing on her face. *So how do I go about it?*

"Right. That and a lot of loving encouragement and prayers."

DJ jerked herself back to pay attention to Bunny. *How rude to run off like that. Thought you were learning better.*

"Are you going to show Herndon this weekend?" Bunny mounted her horse and looked down at DJ.

"I . . . I don't know. Guess I haven't thought that far ahead."

"You're entered, right?"

DJ nodded. "But with Major. And if he's home by the weekend, I need to be here to take care of him."

"This isn't one we stay overnight at." Bunny leaned forward. "DJ, that fall wasn't your fault. Look at me. Hear what I'm saying. It wasn't your fault."

"I . . . I know."

"But you've been beating up on yourself just the same, right?"

How'd you know? DJ looked up at the woman who was becoming her friend. "I'm trying not to."

"What does Bridget say about trying?"

"There is no *try*. There is only *do* or *don't do*, but just trying doesn't cut it."

"Right. Think about that instead." Bunny gathered her reins and signaled her horse to walk. "See you."

"Right." DJ turned and walked toward the barn. *So more practice in thought control. Ugh.*

Riding Herndon took thought control, all right. He shifted with her slightest move. Maybe having a horse that wasn't so responsive had been a blessing after all. She and Major had been learning together, so now she was in catch-up mode all the time. Knowing what Bridget would suggest, DJ spent the time hacking Herndon. They rode circles: walk, trot, halt, canter from a halt, halt from a canter. They trotted serpentines and changed direction, and all the time DJ began to go from head knowledge to soul knowledge that the horse she had under her was not only a gift from her father but one from her heavenly Father as well. Herndon was a horse of her future dreams, only she had him now.

Every time someone said something to her, it broke her concentration and thus Herndon's.

"Am I ready for a horse like him?" she asked Bridget back in her office after she finished riding and grooming the big gelding.

"You will be. Getting used to a new horse takes time and

patience both with yourself and with him. In your case, mostly with yourself."

"But I didn't feel so much like this when I rode him up at Brad's."

"Then you were having fun, not training with him. That makes a big difference in outlook and attitude. Besides, keep in mind that you will not be friends with all your horses like you are with Major. He can read your mind and you his. Some horses are like some people, transparent and all heart. Major is one of those, and I believe you are, too. That means you get hurt easily and hurt for others. I do not want you to ever change that, but you must learn to control it somewhat." She leaned forward, her arms crossed on her desk. "Tender and tough is the way I heard it described. Tender on the inside and tough on the outside. Do you understand?"

DJ shrugged. She kept her hands tucked under her thighs because a discussion like this made her want to chew her fingernails. She rubbed one cuticle with another finger and felt the roughness. But if she could get over biting her fingernails and master algebra, she could handle this. "I . . . I guess so." She ran her tongue over her teeth as she kept her gaze on Bridget. "At least I think I understand, but knowing and doing are so far apart they aren't even in the same country."

Bridget smiled and leaned back. "Ah, out of the mouths of babes. DJ, people fight with that concept all of their lives. Some handle it, others do not. Practice. Know first and then practice. What is that Bible verse?" She rolled her eyes to remember. "I know. As a man—or in our case, woman—thinks in her heart, so is she. We have to get things in our hearts first, like you are saying, and then they will become part of us through practice." She removed the pencil she always wore above her right ear, held in place by blond hair confined by a leather clasp, or on show days, in a net-covered bun. Tapping the pencil on her thumb, she studied the girl across the desk from her.

"Remember, you do not have to do this all at once or by yourself."

DJ nodded again, this time blinking back the moisture she felt clogging her throat and burning her eyes. "I better head on home. Thanks, Bridget." She got to her feet and walked toward the door. "See you tomorrow."

"Good. Oh, and tell your father . . ."

DJ stopped and looked over her shoulder. "Which one?"

Bridget tossed her pencil on the desk. "Always a smart mouth." Her smile said she was teasing. "Robert."

"Okay." DJ waited.

"Tell him I think I may have found a pony for the boys. If he wants me to, I could go with him to look at it."

"Yes!" DJ pumped the air with her arm. "Good thing he's got the men started on the barn." She felt a wriggle start at her toes and work its way up. "Wait till the twins hear this." She trotted out to her bike, throwing in a jump or two along the way just to let off steam.

A song caught her on the bike ride home and she sang it at the top of her lungs. " 'God is so good. God is so good. God is so good, He's so good to me.' " She waved back at a driver who gave her a thumbs-up sign. By the time she parked her bike in the garage she was out of breath from singing and pedaling at the same time.

"Boy, you sound happy." Lindy stood at the counter, munching on a handful of baby carrots. She'd changed out of her work suit and into jean shorts and a T-shirt. Reaching an arm out, she snagged her daughter around the shoulders and gave her a hug.

DJ leaned into her mother's embrace for a moment, then stepped back. "You won't believe what's gone on."

"Try me." Lindy crossed to the refrigerator, pulled out two sodas, and motioned to the deck. "Care to join me?"

"Sure. Let me change first."

Lindy shook her head. "Come on. Guess I can handle a bit of eau de horse. That, at least, won't make me throw up, I don't think."

DJ studied her mother. Makeup didn't cover the shadows under her eyes or the pale cast of her skin. "You all right?" She took the proffered soda and popped the top, taking a sip of mostly fizz.

"Just tired. They say the first three to four months are the hardest, and after that I'm supposed to feel great. I think I've totally forgotten what being pregnant is like. Of course, I was only a kid myself when I carried you." Lindy sank down in the flower-covered cushion of the green iron lounger. "Now, tell me your wonderful news."

They talked for the next half hour and might have gone on longer if the boys hadn't come barreling out and thrown themselves on their mother and older sister.

"We got to pound nails."

"And pick up wood. Mr. Aldon said we could burn it in the fireplace this winter." Bobby looked up at his mother. "Can we?"

Lindy ruffled his blond bowl-cut hair. "Or maybe have a fire in the pit." She nodded toward the bricked-in circle that was part of the deck.

DJ knew it was Bobby because he had a scratch on his right hand. Besides, he always spoke first and never in less than a shout. Billy snuggled up to her side.

"Queenie chewed on a stick. How come she doesn't get slivers in her mouth?"

DJ shrugged. "I don't know." She hugged the little boy closer. "You come up with the hardest questions."

"Just like someone else I know used to and still does." Lindy sipped her soda and chewed another carrot.

"We's hungry," Bobby hinted.

"Go ask Maria for some carrots. Ask her to please bring a tray out here for all of us."

"I want cheese." Billy sat up.

"Me too." DJ gave him a gentle shove. "Get going, Bs."

"Don't ruin your dinner," Lindy called after their hurtling bodies.

"We's not."

DJ leaned back against the cushioned recliner. "This is so fine out here. What smells so good?" She sniffed again.

"The roses over there on the railing, I think." Lindy nodded to the blossoms that looked almost like fire with their combinations of red, yellow, and orange. "I was just getting interested in the garden . . ." She paused. "Now I won't have time again."

They heard Queenie barking at the front door.

"Robert must be home."

The squeals of "Daddy's home!" and pounding feet of the twins on their way to the front door confirmed her comment.

DJ crossed her ankles. "So why don't you start a business here at home and not go to work?" She studied the rim of her soda can, almost afraid to look at her mother.

"Great idea!" Robert set the boys back on their feet and bent to kiss his wife. "How's my favorite pregnant lady?"

"Better." Lindy sucked in a deep breath and let it all out. She patted the cushion beside her knees, and Robert sat down.

"Sorry I interrupted your conversation. Hi, DJ, how was your day?"

"Wait until you hear." Lindy stroked Robert's hand.

After DJ recounted all that had gone on, Robert turned with a smile back to his wife. "So what do you think of DJ's great idea?"

"What, that I quit work?"

"M-hm."

DJ could see he had his fingers crossed down by his leg. She hid her smile behind another drink.

"Are you guys ganging up on me?"

"Us?" Robert gave DJ an innocent look. "Now, DJ, would *we* do that?"

Would my mother really quit work? The thought seemed impossible.

"You could help me and Amy with our business."

"I'm thinking about it. And the book on kids who are entrepreneurs."

DJ felt her chin bounce on her chest. She looked up at Robert, who must have been wearing the same look she was feeling. His thumb and forefinger formed a circle as he leaned forward and kissed his wife again.

DJ pushed herself upright. "Think I'll go see a man about a horse if you two are going to get all mushy." She headed for the open doorway, sure they hadn't heard a word she said.

"You don't need another horse," her mother called as DJ entered the house.

DJ felt the chuckle keep bubbling in her throat as she slapped her leg for Queenie to follow her.

"Dinner in half hour," Maria called after her.

Now to check on Major. Would he be jealous of all the time she had to spend with Herndon now? She jogged up the stairs. She hadn't even thought of him for hours. What kind of friend was she?

11

"HE'S RUNNING A TEMPERATURE," the vet's assistant told DJ over the phone. "We've started him on antibiotics."

"Is this normal?" DJ felt a stab of fear. *What can be wrong with Major now?*

"Not exactly normal, but not unusual, either. The sooner we get him walking around the better, even if he has to hobble."

"But won't that make his shoulder worse?" DJ pressed her ear against the phone, holding it on her shoulder as she paced the room. She had to be careful not to trip on the cord, but she felt too restless to sit down or lie on the bed. "Any idea when we can come and get him?"

"Day after tomorrow, Dr. Jones said. That is if nothing further goes wrong."

DJ thanked the young woman and hung up. She could hear the boys pounding up the stairs. No doubt they'd be at her door in a second or two. "God, please take care of Major." She couldn't think of another word to say. Only *please* repeated itself over and over, like hoofbeats trotting over the cavalletti.

When the boys exploded into her room, she smacked the heel of her hand on her forehead. She'd forgotten to tell

Robert about the pony. "What's up?"

"We's got the table set. Mommy asked if you was cleaned up yet."

DJ shook her head. "But I will be pretty quick if you go on back downstairs."

"Okay." Away they went, Queenie yipping at their heels. Quiet certainly wasn't part of their life. Or anyone else's when they were around.

The yell they sent up when she gave Robert the message made her clap her hands over her ears.

"We's getting a pony, we's getting a pony." They danced and sang while Robert shook his head.

"You think they're excited or what?"

"Mostly what." Lindy made a shushing motion with her hands, and the boys lowered the decibel level by about half.

"When can we go see him?" Bobby climbed up in his father's lap.

"Now?" Billy took the other leg.

"Nope. But I'll talk it over with Ms. Sommersby and let you know." He turned to DJ, an arm around each of the boys. "What did they say about Major?"

Robert shook his head when she told them. "We need to get him home, that's for sure. If vet hospitals are anything like human hospitals, there are all kinds of germs floating around there."

"Poor Major." The boys did their unison thing again.

"Dinner's ready," Maria announced from the doorway. "DJ, please help me carry it out."

DJ did as asked, and as soon as they were all seated, Robert nodded to Billy to say grace.

DJ kept her groan from going past her lips. Billy, as usual, blessed everything but the flowers blooming in the yard.

"Thank you, son," Robert said, but DJ could tell he was having a hard time keeping a straight face. It was the "bless the yellow jackets that are hungry, too" that about did them in.

Bet he won't be blessing the one that stings him. DJ wisely kept her thoughts to herself.

Having dinner out on the deck made DJ give an extra wiggle in her chair. She loved eating outside under the canopy of the oak tree. But while she took part in the conversation, her mind flew to Major's side. *He needs me, and I need to see him to make sure things aren't worse than they are saying.*

"DJ, calling DJ."

Robert's voice jerked her back to the table. "Huh?"

"I said, please pass the butter."

"Oh." She did as asked. So much for controlling her mind. It just zoomed off whether she gave it permission or not.

When they finished eating, Robert handed her the Bible. "Why don't you read for us tonight? The place is marked in the gospel of Matthew."

DJ nodded and flipped the pages.

"Begin with chapter six, verse twenty-five."

DJ began reading. " 'Therefore I tell you, do not be anxious about your life, what you shall eat or what you shall drink, nor about your body, what you shall put on. Is life not more than food, and the body more than clothing.' " DJ wanted to stop right there and think about what was said, but she continued, finishing with, " 'Therefore do not be anxious about tomorrow, for tomorrow will be anxious for itself. Let the day's own trouble be sufficient for the day.' "

DJ shook her head when she finished reading. "Did you choose that section on purpose?" She looked up at Robert.

"Nope, it was on the list I've been using. Why?"

"Just says what I needed to hear."

"Meaning?"

"I've been worrying about Major and thinking I needed to take care of him."

"And?"

"And I just got reminded that God loves him, too, and can take better care of my horse than I can."

"Wise words, my girl. You're learning."

"It's easier to read it than to do it." Lindy laid a hand on the shoulder of the wriggling boy next to her. While he quieted, she motioned him into her lap. The other twin followed suit and climbed up in his father's lap.

"That's for sure." Robert rested his chin on his son's head. "But worry is an elevator going nowhere. You get stuck in it."

"But what's the difference between worrying and just thinking about it?" DJ moved her knife and fork around on her plate.

"Good question." Robert thought for a moment, then glanced at his wife. "Feel free to jump in anytime."

Lindy shrugged. "You're doing fine."

"I guess worrying is more like not being able to think about anything else. Whatever it is that's troubling you seems to take over. You start thinking of all the bad things that could happen, and the more you think about it, the worse it gets."

"Hmm." DJ scraped at a bit of leftover tomato sauce on her plate.

"I heard a man say worry was stewin' without doin'." Lindy kissed the top of the head of the boy cuddled in her lap. Bobby looked up at her, smiled, and snuggled back down.

"I guess when I figure I'm worrying about something, I do like the boys here. I just climb up in my Father's lap and let Him take over."

Bobby sat up straight and looked at his father, his mouth in an O. "You sit on Grandpa's lap?"

Robert shook his head, his eyes sparkling. "Leave it to you, the literal one. No, I meant my heavenly Father."

"You sit in *God's* lap?" The other twin's mouth matched the first.

"Time out!" Robert used both hands to make the referee's signal. He turned to Maria, who, like DJ and Lindy, was trying not to laugh. "What are we having for dessert?"

"Cookies and ice cream."

"Good. Let's have it. Bobby, Billy, you help Maria clear off the dishes."

The boys slid off the laps, and Bobby turned to his father. "We didn't pray."

"We will. Get moving." Robert tried to give DJ and her mother a stern look—and failed. "And don't either of you bring up worrying again, you hear, at least not tonight."

DJ looked at her mother, and both of them caught the giggles.

" 'Consider the lilies of the field, they neither toil nor spin . . .' " Lindy looked at her husband. Laughing, she laid a hand on his forearm. "Robert, you make me so happy."

"Me too." As she said it, DJ realized how happy she truly was.

The meeting of the business club after school on Wednesday opened with a retired businesswoman from the Small Business Administration ready to discuss the greeting card business now called DJAM, Etc. All the kids liked the name.

"First off, let me say what a marvelous business I think this is and what a good example of entrepreneurship for all of us." Mrs. Enrico smiled at Amy and DJ sitting in the front row. "You are two talented young women and"—she sent her smile out to the rest of the fifteen kids in the room—"with the help of the rest of you, there can be great things ahead. Now, I've read all the information Mr. Mann gave me, so let's hear what your committees have accomplished this last week."

Each of the committees made their reports to applause and more lively discussion.

"I'm impressed." Mrs. Enrico smiled at everyone again, her dark eyes sparkling. "I wish I'd had all of you helping me when I started my business twenty years ago." She took a stack of papers from the desk behind her. "Will someone hand these out for me, please?"

As one of the students did that, she continued. "Now, most businesses go belly-up for lack of capital, so I'm showing you a simplified business plan, the kind of form you would need to fill out if you were going to a bank to borrow money. They want to make sure you'll be able to pay back your loan."

Everyone chuckled at the face she made. "But there are other ways to finance a business. Anyone have any ideas what that may be?"

"Borrow from your parents."

"Ask your grandparents."

"Earn the money some other way."

She nodded. "Those could work. It all depends on how much money you need." She looked at DJ and Amy. "How have you been getting the money you need so far?"

"We make our cards, sell them, and then we have money to make more."

"Right. That's the best way when you have a good product to sell. But what if you got an order for, let's say, five hundred packets?"

DJ and Amy looked at each other and shrugged.

"How much would you need?"

Both girls fumbled for paper and pencil, but before they'd gotten started, a boy from the back of the room called out the amount. He held up his calculator and grinned at them.

By the end of the meeting, the group had decided that they would like to continue working with this project, even through the summer and into the next school year.

"Thanks for your help," DJ said to Mrs. Enrico. "My mother has been giving us suggestions, too. I wish she had come today."

"Please, feel free to call me anytime. I'd love to keep track of how you do. Mr. Mann does a really great job with this business club. Why, I know of a couple businesses that came from his group in the past and are still going. There's one that two boys put together with computer games, and they've made a killing with it. They're millionaires and aren't even twenty-five yet."

"Wow. Then I could buy all the horses I wanted."

Amy rolled her eyes. "There *are* other things in life besides horses."

"So?" DJ grinned. "And I better get going or I'll be late for my lesson. Thanks again." She waved at Mr. Mann and turned to answer a question from one of the girls on the promotion committee.

"The reporter from the *Contra Costa Times* business section will be calling you about an interview. Her name is Rhonda Ewing. It will be up to you to set up a time," a dark-haired girl said.

DJ and Amy swapped *wow* looks, along with question-mark eyebrows.

"What'll we say?" DJ gulped.

"I think I'm gonna throw up."

Mrs. Enrico stopped beside them. "All you have to do is be yourselves and you'll do fine. I have one suggestion, though. Think about why you started your business and where you want it to go. You might write those things down so it gets real clear in your mind."

On the way out to meet Joe, DJ turned to Amy. "You get the feeling that building a business like we're doing is like just about anything else?"

"Huh?" Amy's face said the same.

"Well, Bridget says you have to know where you are going, focus, and write your dreams down, doesn't she?"

"Yeah."

"Well?" DJ shrugged.

"I guess. But I don't like—"

"Don't like what?"

"Well, answering questions like that. You do it, and I'll back you up."

"Get real, Ames. Wait until I tell Mom."

"Good, let *her* talk to the reporter." The two girls waved at Joe waiting for them in his Explorer.

"Sheesh." DJ settled back against the seat after telling her grandfather what had happened. "Joe, what do you think?"

"I think you two are pretty remarkable young women, and I'll tell any reporter that any day of the week." He stopped at Amy's house. "You want us to wait?"

"No, thanks, I'll ride my bike." Amy slammed the door behind her and waved.

"Phone call for you." Maria pointed to the message pad by the phone when DJ entered the kitchen. "I say you call back."

DJ read the message. The reporter had called. If her stomach did flip-flops like this at the idea of an interview, what would it do the day they met? *Maybe I just won't call back.* She glared at herself, snagged the paper off the pad, and headed for her room. She'd better call right now before she chickened out.

Her hands still shook a few minutes later as she hung up the phone. The reporter would come to her house on Monday after school and planned on interviewing Mr.

Mann for more information about the two girls and maybe another story about the success of the school's business class.

"Good, then we won't be the only ones to have to answer questions." DJ shucked her school clothes and pulled on her barn jeans and T-shirt. Grabbing her boots, she jogged in her stockinged feet back downstairs and into the kitchen for something to eat before leaving for the Academy.

"Dinner at 6:30." Maria nodded toward the clock.

"I might be late, since I'm getting over there late."

"You be here." Maria continued grating cheese. "Enchiladas tonight. *Muy bueno.*"

"You make everything very good." DJ waved her apple, then clamped it in her teeth and, leaning against the wall by the door, pulled on her boots. She walked out the door just as Joe drove back in the yard.

"The vet said to call around noon tomorrow to see if Major can come home. I'll ask Mom if I can go along." She gave her grandfather an innocent look. "Unless you can't go tomorrow?"

"Oh, I can go, but you can't, so don't bother getting your mother all het up."

"GJ, please."

"Uh-uh. Mel said she'd go along. We plan on a nice early lunch, then pick up the horse and drive home before the traffic hits. You'll be working Herndon by the time we get back. I already checked with Mrs. Yamamoto, and she will pick you two up after school. Now, aren't you proud of your old grandpa for taking care of all this?"

DJ wanted to cross her arms and stick out her tongue. "But . . ."

"Nope. No argument is going to work, so forget it. Major's been through worse."

"But it wasn't my fault before." She muttered the words under her breath.

"I'm going to pretend I didn't hear that. And you can pretend you didn't say it, let alone think it. Okay?" He stopped the truck in the shade of the Academy barn and turned to look at her. "Ah, DJ, learning to not blame yourself is a hard lesson, one that you have to go over again and again. There is no easy way out of this except to keep going over it until you learn to let God handle the judging. And He won't blame you, so let it go."

"I'm trying." DJ studied her tattered cuticle. Her fingernails needed cutting. "You think Mom will let me spend the night here to take care of him?"

"I wouldn't ask."

"I guess not." She glanced up, feeling her grandfather's warm gaze on her face. "Do you ever play 'what if' or blame yourself?"

"Yep. But I'm trying to quit that, too, and let me tell you, I've been trying a whole lot longer than you."

"Then . . . then . . ."

"Then why try?"

She nodded.

"Because I'd probably be dead of a heart attack or stroke or something if I worried like I used to or blamed myself for the accidents or figured everything was all my fault. Darla Jean Randall, you are far ahead of me in learning these things, and I'm grateful you ask me questions like this. Now let go and let God."

"Let God what?"

"Let Him be God and you be Darla Jean, one of his favorite daughters."

DJ left the truck with his words winding through her heart and mind. *Let God, huh?* Somehow the thought that her grandfather struggled with some of the same things she did made her feel comforted. She picked up a grooming bucket on her way past the tack room, along with treats for Herndon.

"Hi, big guy." Herndon extended his nose to sniff her pockets. "Ah, getting into the habit, huh?" She gave him half a horse cookie, followed by a carrot. With her hands empty, she stroked down his long nose and up around his dark ears. His muzzle had light brown hairs that deepened to black ears and mane. A few white hairs formed a little whorl midway between his eyes.

"You know what? You are one fine-looking horse, and I am proud to know that you are mine. What do you think?" His ears flicked back and forth, and he sniffed her hands again.

Outside of his stall, in the barn alley, she snapped the cross-ties in place and began grooming the sleek, dark hide, more black than bay. With both hands occupied with brushes, she kept jerking her mind back to what she was doing when it wanted to head on over to the vet hospital and check on Major. When Herndon was so shiny he looked like he'd been sprayed with water, DJ led him out to the hot walker to burn off some energy while she shoveled out the latest droppings. She could tell Joe had cleaned the stall that morning.

By the time Herndon was saddled and she'd warmed him up, Bridget was standing at the gate, talking with Bunny.

"I will be ready in a minute, DJ. You go on and warm up over the jumping grid."

But by the end of the lesson, when DJ and Herndon were both dripping, all she could think was how far they had to go to become a team—and how much she missed Major.

The next afternoon, before she worked with Herndon, she stopped by Bridget's office.

"You got a minute?"

"For you, yes." Bridget pushed her glasses up on her forehead. "What do you need?"

"It's about this weekend. Do you think I should show Herndon or just cancel?"

"What do you think?"

"I'd rather stay here and take care of Major."

"This would be a good first show with Herndon. As we have said in the past, the more you show, the better you will become."

DJ nodded. "I was afraid that's what you would say."

"Then why did you ask?"

DJ shrugged and thought a moment. "I . . . I just don't feel comfortable with him yet. Like . . . I'm always just a tiny bit behind." She spread her thumb and forefinger apart about an inch. "And if he refuses a jump, I'll about die." There, she'd said it, one of her worst fears. The airborne feeling from Major going down shuddered up her spine. *What if Herndon got hurt, too?*

DJ WAS RIGHT. SHE HATED to leave Major again.

"He'll be all right." Joe rubbed his old horse's ears. "He's a bit skinnier, but then, he was getting fat."

"He was not." DJ laid her palm on her horse's shoulder. Still hot to the touch and tender. But at least he had quit shaking. The brief walk from trailer to stall gave him the shakes so bad, DJ's teeth rattled. She rubbed in the liniment, murmuring comfort all the time. "Brad said he'd bring down his ultrasound machine to help reduce the swelling."

"Don't worry, kid, we got stuff here to help him be more comfortable." Joe hefted the sack of anti-inflammatories and pain-killers. "And those ultrasound machines are pretty impressive. A doctor used one on me one time, and I healed twice as fast."

Major snuffled her hair and blew carrot breath in her face. His whiskers tickled and made her smile. "You old lover, you." She wrapped both arms around his neck and felt him sigh. He braced his weight on three legs, the front one cocked. "I wish there were more I could do to help you." She looked at Joe. "What if he tries to lie down tonight and can't get up? He'll hurt it worse."

"He's too smart for that, aren't you, old man?" Major

cocked his head so Joe could continue to rub his ear.

"Don't call him old." DJ stepped back. "I've got to work Herndon, Major, and then I'll be back. You be good now."

"And I've got to move the truck." Joe had backed the trailer through the barn so Major had only to hobble down the gently sloped ramp and right into his stall.

"You think we should cross-tie him so he won't move around?"

Joe shook his head. "You've got to give him credit, DJ. He knows how much his shoulder hurts and that walking makes it worse."

DJ kissed Major's nose and gave him one last pat. "See ya, fella."

He nickered as she left the stall. It took all the strength she could muster to go back down the aisle to Herndon's stall inside the barn. While the big horse watched her, his nostrils never moved in either a soundless nicker or a vocal welcoming one. His ears pricked the closer she walked, and he finally reached for the treat he already knew would be in her pocket.

Don't be stupid, her little voice reminded her. *You haven't had him long enough for him to love you like Major does. Besides, remember, some horses by nature aren't affectionate. Just like some people aren't.*

But the urge to return to Major made her grit her teeth.

"I do think you should go ahead with Saturday's show," Bridget said later. "The more time you spend with Herndon, the better."

Guilt made her stomach twinge. Major needed her, Herndon did not. Afraid that all her thoughts were like a video across her face, she nodded. "I will. Who else is going?"

Bridget handed her the day's schedule. "At least you will not have to leave at daybreak. And you can come home as soon as you are finished."

"I guess."

"DJ, Major will get better." Bridget's voice took on a softer note. "I know you are concerned about him, but you cannot let that interfere with your work."

DJ nodded and let out a sigh that made her shoulders slump. She nibbled her bottom lip, then looked up at her coach. "You think I will ever love Herndon like I do Major?"

"I think so, yes. But there is something special about the first horse you ever own. And that is good. Major has a unique place in your heart, but with love, there is always room for more. And the more you give, the more you get." She leaned forward. "Give it time, DJ. Give it time."

The show on Saturday went okay. At least she didn't end up on Herndon's neck, and the ribbons they brought home from Hunter on the Flat and Hunter Over Jumps did help her feel a bit better. Herndon had class, that's for sure, and he loved the show-ring. The low bars on the jumps hadn't bothered them much, but she could still feel him hesitate. Not trusting her horse gave her a headache by the end of the day. *This, too, will change.* She repeated the promise to herself several times in the hopes she would begin to believe it.

"We's going to see our pony, we's going to see the pony." The boys' chanting when DJ came in the door after the show didn't help her headache any.

"Okay, okay, give me a minute." She knew by the hurt looks on their faces that her tone had been sharper than she intended. "Sorry, guys." She ruffled their hair and touched their noses with one finger. "Let me put my show stuff away and I'll be right back down."

"We was waiting for you." They wore matching kicked-puppy looks.

Guilt again. This time it tightened the vise around her head.

"DJ, what's wrong?" Lindy strolled out of the living room, her finger holding the place in the book she'd been reading.

"I've got a headache, that's all." DJ rubbed her neck.

"That's not like you."

"I know, but . . ." DJ scrinched her eyes closed. "Let me get something and I'll be ready to go." The thought of all the homework piled on top of her desk made her groan inside. She'd planned to get that paper that was due Monday done last night, but it was taking a lot longer than she thought.

"I'll sit in back with you and rub your neck. That might help," Lindy called up the stairs after her daughter.

DJ swallowed a pill and changed her clothes, eyeing both the bed and the Jacuzzi. No time for either, but they sure looked appealing. She and late nights just didn't do too well, but she didn't dare tell her mother that.

Once they were all in the car and on the way, Lindy did as she promised. With strong fingers she massaged the tight cords in DJ's neck and down into her shoulders. "Let your head fall forward," she said softly, all the while working out the kinks and knotted muscles.

"Oh, Mom, that feels wonderful." DJ let her eyes drift closed.

"Better?"

"Mmm."

DJ woke up again when the car stopped. She raised her head from off her mother's shoulder and blinked at the downing sun shining in her eyes. "Where are we?"

"To see our pony." Bobby leaned over the front seat. "Come on."

The pony was everything Bridget had said: good confirmation, friendly, and well trained. Thirteen hands tall.

"Our daughter showed him for years, but now she has graduated to a larger horse and we want a good home for him." The woman patted the black-and-white paint pony.

"We were told he's Welsh and Arab, but we're not sure what gave him the paint coloring," she said in answer to DJ's question. "General is smart and loves little kids. I've never had a moment's worry when Janny was with him." She raised her eyebrows. "With her horse now, though, it's different. He's a handful."

The boys took turns riding with DJ leading, then DJ let out the stirrups and rode General herself.

"Janny rode him both English and Western, and he's flashy enough that he did well."

"We'll talk it over and get back to you," Robert said when DJ dismounted. After her own horse, she'd felt as if she was on a tricycle.

"D-a-d-d-y." The boys groaned at the same time.

Robert looked at DJ. "What do you think?"

"I think he'd do fine. Bridget thought so, too."

Robert gave Lindy the same questioning look. She nodded and shrugged.

"For what I know about horses, why not?"

"I guess we all agree, then." He dug in his pocket for his checkbook to the shrieks of delight from the boys.

"My dad will be back tomorrow to pick him up." Robert paused before writing any more. "Are the saddle and bridle for sale, too?"

"Sure, and his blanket if you want." The woman named another figure.

Robert nodded again. "Good, might as well get it all."

DJ looked at her mother, who gave a slight shrug. *I'll*

never get used to this, buying something without having to save and work extra hard. You'd think the boys would be spoiled rotten, but they're not.

Lindy, having read DJ's thoughts, put her arm around her shoulder. "It's nice, though, isn't it?"

DJ nodded.

With the boys finally settling down, halfway home they stopped for ice-cream cones. "To celebrate," as Robert said.

"Celebrate what?" Lindy asked around licking her pistachio almond cone.

"We've got lots to celebrate. DJ, what about you?"

She thought a moment. "Major is doing better." Another thought. "And I didn't end up on Herndon's neck today."

"Or the ground," her mother added with a shudder. "I'm glad I wasn't there last week. Just picturing you flying through the air almost makes me throw up."

"Everything makes you throw up." Robert gave her a teasing glance.

Lindy punched him in the shoulder. "I didn't this morning. I can celebrate that."

"We's gots a pony." The boys bounced on the car seat as they said it together.

"So what are you celebrating?" Lindy looked at Robert and licked a dribble off her finger.

She's so different. The thought made DJ realize she had that as something else to celebrate.

"I'm celebrating my family, a wife who throws up when I kiss her in the morning, a daughter who takes headers off horses, two boys who out-do the Energizer Bunny, and a baby on the way. What more could a man ask for?"

"D-a-d!"

"Daddy!"

"Robert!"

They all answered at the same time. DJ couldn't believe she'd said that. But he was her dad, and it felt good to call him so. She looked up to catch his gaze in the mirror. His eyes were shining.

"Thanks, DJ."

Lindy reached across the back of the front seat and patted her daughter's knee.

When DJ pleaded to be able to stay home from dinner out and a family drive in order to work on her homework after church Sunday afternoon, things weren't quite as sunny.

"Are you behind?" Lindy asked.

"Not really, but I've got a paper to write and a book report to finish. Plus regular stuff. Finals start in a week."

"Sorry, DJ. We'll miss you." Robert tossed a jacket to his wife. "I'd like for you to plan on time with all of us on the few Sunday afternoons you aren't at a horse show." A frown formed a V between his eyebrows. "Your grades are holding up, aren't they?"

DJ nodded. "And I'm trying to keep them that way." She wasn't even riding today. Didn't they understand that? "Sorry." She felt like she'd kicked the puppy again at the looks on the boys' faces.

Brad called that evening. DJ had been attacked by the groggies by that time.

"So what have you decided about the horse camp in New Jersey? We need to get on that."

DJ rubbed her forehead. "I don't know."

"Do you want to go?"

"Yes, but . . ."

Brad waited. "But?"

"I don't know how I'm going to get it all in. Summer school, art school, all the shows, Mom and Robert want me to go on a vacation with the family, the USET, how do I do it all?"

"Guess you'll have to pick and choose. Let me know as soon as you can."

"Okay." She hung up feeling Brad wasn't too happy with her right now. But then, what was new? At the rate she was going, she had everyone but Gran upset with her, and if she decided not to do art classes in summer school, that would change, too.

DJ eyed the letter propped up against one of her horse statues. Ms. Isabella Gant wrote to invite her to attend the drawing seminar she was offering at the Arts College in San Francisco in July. After the fantastic time she'd had at the last one, she really wanted to do that again.

And Amy was planning on the weeklong pack trip up in the Sierra Mountains that the Academy put on every year. DJ shook her head. She could just see Herndon up in the mountains. Get real. But she could have gone with Major. At least he'd been happy to see her when she pedaled over to feed him that afternoon.

"Our pony is at Grandpa and Grandma's," the boys informed her when they came home. "Until Daddy finishes the barn and fences." They stood beside her desk, eyeing the Jelly Bellys she'd stashed for homework energy.

"Help yourselves, but only a couple."

They let the rest of their handfuls slide back into the dish.

"We missed you."

"I missed you, too, but now I have to get this done, okay?" She waited, hoping they would take the hint.

"Bobby, Billy, you let DJ study." Her mother's voice floated up the stairs.

"Bye."

"See ya." DJ gave a sigh of relief. Searching out a tutti fruiti candy, she put it on her tongue and sucked.

She turned out her light at midnight, with the paper done, but not the book report. When did she have enough extra time to read the remaining hundred pages, no matter how good the book was?

By the time school was out Monday, the butterflies were climbing up her throat, then jumping off like kids into a lake.

"I think I'm going to be sick," Amy said with a groan.

"Me too. Let's run away." DJ tossed her backpack onto the floor of Joe's car.

"You two look like you lost your last friend, but how can that be when you're together?"

"That reporter from the paper is coming to interview us."

"Oh, that's right. The way you look, I'd think she was coming to shoot you."

"Funny."

"Might as well be." Amy rolled her eyes. "I'd rather clean stalls any day."

"You like cleaning stalls. I'd rather do algebra."

A strange car was already parked in the driveway.

"Joe, please, drive us somewhere else." DJ moaned. "Now I *know* I'm going to be sick."

WORRYING ABOUT SOMETHING is always worse than doing it. Or fearing it.

"There, that wasn't so bad," Lindy said with a smile at each of the girls. The newspaper woman had just left.

"I guess." DJ looked at Amy. "Did I sound like a complete idiot or what?"

"Me too."

"No, you did good."

"Sure, and the zit on my chin is going to glow like a lightbulb in that picture." Amy, who rarely had a zit, fingered the offending swelling.

"Well, I think you did a good job, and this will be great publicity. I know businesspeople who would be willing to pay lots of bucks for coverage like this." Lindy stood and stretched. "I think I'll walk over and get the boys. Gran must be serving milk and cookies right about now."

"You wouldn't like to run us up to the Academy, would you? Amy doesn't have a bike here."

Lindy shrugged. "Sure, why not. Although a run over there wouldn't hurt you."

DJ checked her Winnie-the-Pooh watch. "I've got class in twenty minutes. Zowie, I better get moving." DJ charged up the stairs to change.

Herndon didn't like being rushed. He shifted from side to side when she groomed him and sidestepped all the way to the arena.

"Herndon, stand still." DJ repeated the command when the gelding took a couple of steps while she was trying to mount. He moved again.

She clamped a hand on the reins under his jaw and glared at him. "You stand still, hear me?"

"He is just reacting to you," Bridget said as she opened the gate and walked through.

DJ knew she was right. She'd been racing around, doing everything at top speed, and all it cost her was a flighty horse and sweaty armpits. She took in a deep breath herself, let it out, and stroked Herndon's face, down his cheeks, and up around his ears. He tilted his head slightly to the side to make it easier for her to reach his favorite spot and sighed, too.

"I'm sorry, big fella. I know better, but I was running late." Herndon's eyes drifted closed, and he rested his forehead against her chest.

"Just like magic, huh?" Bridget left the arena. "See you out at the jump in ten minutes. I have some things I can do while you warm him up, now that you have him cooled down." Her laugh drifted behind her.

DJ mounted with smooth grace and moved Herndon into a walk, then a slow trot. But while she thought they were both calmed down, out in the jumping ring, Herndon ran out. When she brought him up to the jump again, he did the same.

"Okay, we will now go back to the basics." Bridget put all the bars on the ground, and DJ spent the hour trotting around and around, over the cavalletti and crossrails and around again. If she heard "Focus, keep him between your hands and your legs," one more time, she thought she might scream. She jogged home after giving Major another treatment just to wear off her frustration. Frustration she didn't dare show when Bridget was around.

"Mom, can I take my dinner upstairs so I can get on the books?"

"I guess." Lindy took another look at her daughter. "What's the matter?"

"Herndon kept running out, so we did the 'basics.' " She put a sneer on the B word. "That horse might drive me to . . . to . . . I don't know what."

"How's Major?"

"That old sweetie, he'd never act like this. He's getting better. He puts some weight on that foot now. I thought you were going for the boys."

"Mother asked if they could have dinner there so Joe could teach them how to groom General. I'm not sure who is having more fun with that pony, him or the boys." Lindy looked around the kitchen. "Since Robert won't be home until late, why don't you bring your books down here, and we'll eat out on the deck? Just the two of us. Maria went to see her sister."

"Okay."

Comfortable on the loungers, they both read their books while they ate. Queenie crawled up by DJ and stretched out by her crossed legs.

"Darla Jean, you better come in before you get too cold." Lindy touched her daughter's shoulder.

DJ opened her eyes and blinked, then blinked again. "Oh . . . what happened?" She looked around for her book and pushed off the throw that now covered her.

"You fell asleep." Lindy sat down on the other lounger and faced her daughter. "If you are this tired, something has to give. How long since you went to bed at a decent hour?"

DJ shrugged and pulled the fleece throw back up around her shoulders. Queenie licked her hand, so DJ stroked the dog's silky head.

"Okay, this is what I propose. You cut back on classes—"

"But, Mom!"

"Only until school is out. And that Arab show that is coming up this weekend is out."

"But I told Brad I'd—"

"I already talked with him. He called about the USET thing. He agrees with me that your studies and your health come first. You can take care of the horses and exercise Herndon, but for the next two weeks, only one class a week and the one you teach. That will give you study time, and I want the lights out at 10:00."

DJ glared at her mother, but the yawn that made her jaw crack lessened the impact. As if a glare would do any good. She pushed back the throw and got to her feet. "Thanks a lot."

Sarcasm didn't work, either. Lindy stood and, taking the throw from DJ's hands, put it around her shoulders. "I'll bring you some hot chocolate, or would you rather have a soda?"

"Orange soda." With Queenie Velcroed to her knee, DJ climbed the stairs to her room, yawning twice along the way. She'd slept for two hours. She glared at the face in the bathroom mirror. "Sheesh, you dope." But the circles under her eyes made her look like a raccoon, and she knew it.

The days leading to finals fell over each other in their rush to get past.

On Sunday night Brad and Jackie stopped by after he came to pick up the ultrasound machine.

"Thanks so much for letting us use it," DJ said. "It worked like magic. Major is so much better, I can hardly believe it."

"Most likely your love and good care had something to do with it." Brad laid a hand on her shoulder.

"Prayers too." DJ laid her cheek on her father's hand. "Thank you again."

"You are very welcome."

"How about staying for dinner. It'll be ready in just a few minutes." Lindy invited. "Robert will be barbecuing."

So as dusk fell, they were all sitting out on the deck, Gran and Joe included. Talk turned to summer vacation and how they were going to work it all out.

DJ went upstairs and came back down with a paper in her hands. "I wrote down how I think my summer ought to go. You want to hear it?"

"Sure." Robert moved the table lamp over to where she'd sat before.

"As soon as school is out, Amy and I are going to your house for a week, right?" She nodded to Brad and Jackie, who both nodded. "Okay, then I'd like to go to summer school at Mount Diablo Community College for their art courses like Gran suggested. That would be for six weeks in the mornings. I have three shows in those weeks also, including the Arab show you talked about over the Fourth of July weekend." Again DJ nodded at Brad.

"Sounds good," he said.

"Then there is that A-level show in Sacramento, if Herndon and I are ready for it." She glanced back at her paper. "Then I want to go to the class Ms. Gant is teaching. I could take BART in for that every day."

She glanced at her mother, wondering what she would think of DJ's riding the Bay Area Rapid Transit alone. But Lindy just nodded and ran the tip of her tongue around her cheek.

"And after that the USET." She looked from Robert to her mother and back again. "I know you want us all to take a vacation, and I thought maybe the week before school starts again would work."

DJ laid her paper down on the table. The boys were giggling, Queenie yipping at them off in the grass by the jungle gym set Robert had built for them. A bird made a sleepy call in the tree up above, and sprinklers ratcheted in the neighbor's yard.

"Sounds like a good plan to me," Robert said, nodding and reaching for the paper at the same time. "I can tell you put a lot of time and thought into this."

Now it was DJ's turn to nod.

"Doesn't look to me like there is much time here for kicking back."

"No, it sure doesn't." Lindy looked over Robert's shoulder at the list. She looked up at DJ. "You aren't going to try to go on the wilderness pack trip?"

"Can you see Herndon on a trail?"

That brought chuckles from everyone.

"Besides, even if Major were well enough, which I doubt, I just don't have time." While she and Amy had talked about going for the last couple of summers, and two of her girls and their families were going, DJ knew it wasn't for her. At least not this year.

"You'll need time for your card business, too," Lindy reminded her.

"I know. And I want to teach the boys how to ride right, but I can do that in the early afternoons." DJ looked around the group, then lifted her paper up. "So is this all right with everybody?"

"I hope you can spend some more time with us," Jackie added, "although I know we get show times together. Maybe a few days after USET?" She looked at Lindy and Robert for permission.

"Could be." Robert looked over at DJ and nodded. "I think you've done a good job on your plans. Maybe I should hire you in my business."

"Robert!" Lindy play-punched his shoulders.

"Just kidding."

DJ slept around the clock after finals were over on Thursday. She staggered over to the barns to care for the horses that afternoon, returned home, crawled into bed, and slept through the night.

"Welcome back to the land of the living," her mother said the next morning when DJ entered the kitchen.

"What day is this?" DJ stuck her head in the fridge for something to eat. "I'm starved."

"I'm sure you are. I think you forgot to eat last night. When I went up to call you, you were sound asleep again, so I left you alone."

DJ stood up and looked back around the refrigerator door. "If it's Friday, how come you are home?"

"I'm taking a couple of vacation days." Lindy stretched her hands above her head. "That's part of my three-week notice. In fact, I only have one more week in the office."

"You what?"

"I quit my job."

"You did?" DJ slammed the door and did a jig step over to her mother. "Really?"

"I decided you kids needed me at home and I needed to be here. So Maria can have a few extra days off this summer if she wants, and I plan to start my book on young entrepreneurs. You and Amy and that business club have inspired me. Mr. Mann is excited about sharing kids from the last few years with me, too."

"I can't believe this!" DJ put the back of her hand to her forehead. "God, do you hear me? This is like super way cool wonderful."

"Maybe I'll even make a baby quilt for the little one here." Lindy patted her barely rounded belly.

DJ grinned.

Brad picked up DJ and Amy, along with Herndon, on Sunday afternoon. By the time they arrived at Gladstone, his ranch north of San Francisco in Santa Rosa, they'd talked about showing, plans for the summer, USET, and how the card line was coming.

DJ enjoyed pointing out landmarks to Amy, especially those high-water marks left from the flood the winter before.

"I told Stormy you were coming, and she said she was glad—it's been too long since she saw you."

DJ and Amy shook their heads and gave each other *the look*. Stormy was a little filly that DJ helped keep alive when she was born during the flood. The river had taken over the barns, and the horses they couldn't get hauled to higher grounds earlier were kept up by the house since it was on a knoll higher than the rest of the farm. After the flood receded, Brad gave Stormy to DJ as a gift. Stormy now starred in the line of cards through DJ's drawings.

"You think I'm kidding, right?"

"Yep. But that's all right. If you understand horse language that well, we could make a fortune off you."

"You could go on TV," Amy continued with a sober face that twitched with the need to giggle.

"Better'n our cards, huh?"

"All right, you two, rule number one of this week: no picking on the male member of this household."

"Sure, I'll just ask Jackie to make sure this rule is really in effect."

Still laughing, the three of them drove up to the long, white main barn. Herndon walked out of the trailer and stood looking around as if he were glad to be home. He whinnied once and whinnied again when several horses answered him.

"Okay, what did he say that time?"

"Hey, guys, I'm home, so you better watch out."

"Right." DJ led her horse into the barn. "What stall do you want him in?"

"His stall, where else?"

Herndon knew it was home. He walked in as if he owned the place and all the others were his subjects waiting to greet him. Nickers, whinnies, and scuffling feet made DJ and Amy laugh again.

"Where's Stormy?" DJ asked as soon as they had Herndon fed and settled in.

"In the other barn. Come on."

Stormy's mother came right up to get her treats, but Stormy hung back, too big now to hide behind her mother but not taking any chances with the strangers.

"I thought she was excited for me to get here?" DJ nudged Brad with her elbow.

"She said she was. I guess you can't trust the word of a filly." Brad held a horse cookie out for the youngster, but she would have none of it.

"She is so pretty. Look at her, all legs still." Amy rubbed the mare's nose and watched the baby.

"But can she run." Brad held out her treat, and she finally reached forward to snatch it out of his hands. "She's a real show-off. I can't wait for you to take her into the ring.

I'm hoping you can show her at the Arab show in Prescott in July. That would be an ideal show for her, and Jackie's been teaching her manners and to lead like she should. Of course you can't tell that now."

DJ knew she would sit in the corner again and wait for Stormy to come to her. It shouldn't take as long as last time. If only she could come up here more, but life was so busy.

As they reached the house, Brad told them a joke, so the three of them entered the house chuckling.

"Sounds like some happy people who are just in time for dinner." Jackie gave both DJ and Amy a hug. "You know where to put your things. I'm sure glad you are finally here.

"John will be here first thing in the morning to work with you and Herndon," she went on. "I told him you are having trouble jumping, so he's been thinking on it."

"I know it's my fault. I'm just not doing something the way he is used to."

"Not necessarily." Working with a new horse always takes time.

After dinner and cleanup, the four of them ambled back to the barns to check that all was okay. Herndon greeted Jackie with a nicker and toss of the head.

One day, horse, DJ promised herself, *you'll greet me like that.*

But all through the videos and shows and events they watched, DJ fought to ignore the bite of jealousy. After all, Herndon had been Jackie's horse for years.

John Talbot arrived promptly at 9:00 Monday morning. After listening to DJ's tale, he nodded his head. "Let me show you what I think you are doing and how we can make it work." He checked the stirrup length and mounted Herndon. "Riding is a feeling thing," he said with a smile down at the girls. "I call it strength under control. Now, I know you know this, but let me review. Your seat and legs are always driving him forward. Some of the most common problems are uneven reins, being left behind . . ."

DJ nodded at that one. "And I can't seem to change that."

"Or you're dropping him. When you get left behind on one jump, then many times one of your reins gets uneven when you try to get back together. You have to make sure you look where you are going, too, always to the next jump. He will go the way you look."

DJ nodded again. She'd heard all this before with Bridget, but she didn't care. If this man could help her, she'd cheer forever.

"Now, watch carefully. I have a video camera here, so you can see the same thing over and over this afternoon. The moves are hard to see at regular speed." He took Herndon over the three jumps they had set up. "Did you notice how he rounds over the jump? You must, too. Now watch again."

DJ concentrated on watching his hands one time, legs the next, and seat the third.

"Okay, your turn." He dismounted, adjusted the stirrup leathers, and stepped back.

After an hour of working with him, DJ felt like she had cooked spaghetti for legs. Her timing had improved, but she still didn't feel like she had it.

"It will come," Talbot promised. "The two of you are going to be hard to beat one of these days. Just concentrate on the basics. You have to *ride* this horse to get the best out of him, but it's there."

"Herndon," DJ muttered after the trainer left, "if we don't get our act together, we won't be showing next weekend, let alone going to USET." The thought of either or both made her stomach do flips again.

14

"HERE SHE COMES."

"I know."

DJ and Amy lay in the grass in the pasture Saturday afternoon, watching the clouds tagging across the blue sky. They could hear Stormy coming, one foot swishing through the grass, then another. The filly and her two mates inched closer and closer, sniffing at DJ's outflung hand, then her arm.

DJ barely dared to breathe. The whiskers tickled her skin. A dished face with velvet nose and big brown eyes with eyelashes to die for blocked the sun. Stormy sniffed DJ's hair and her face. The filly's whiskers tickled her nose. DJ knew she was going to sneeze and scare them away.

"A—a—choo." The three colts leaped back as if they'd been bit by horseflies.

"Fiddle." DJ sat up and dug in her shorts pocket for a tissue. "Come on, sweetie. We didn't hurt you."

"If only I could have a camera at the ground angle and get that picture. It would be priceless." Amy sat cross-legged and held out her hand. "Come on, Jackson, you can come back now." The near black colt that looked so much like his sire, Matadorian, sidled forward again.

DJ flopped back down. "I don't want to go home to-

141

morrow. I haven't gotten half enough drawing time in, and I'm going to miss Stormy like crazy." The filly came up and nuzzled DJ's hair again, then searched her pockets for goodies. "Sorry, baby, you ate them all. See?" DJ pulled out her pockets. "Not a crumb left."

"I've taken five rolls of film. Can you believe that?"

"Easy. You've lived with the camera glued to your eye." DJ scratched the filly's neck, pulling out the furry baby hair that flew away on the breeze. "Look at this undercoat. She's going to be fiery red." DJ turned to Amy, who played with the other foals. "What am I going to do with her? She can't be a jumper, she won't be big enough."

"Ah, but you'll show her in the Arabian shows, and she'll make a wonderful riding horse. Do you think you'll ever take Herndon up in Briones?"

"Probably not. He's too valuable and too high-strung."

"I rest my case. Or up in the Sierra?"

"I get the point."

"Besides, she'll make a wonderful brood mare someday. Then you can have babies like this to play with every year." Amy tickled the nose of the gray foal with a long blade of grass. "This one is going to be on our cards, you watch."

"I bet the one with them all sound asleep in the grass will be a keeper, too." DJ got to her feet. "Come on, I'm hungry." She checked her watch. "And I have another lesson in an hour."

"I hate to take you home again," Brad said Sunday as they neared Briones Academy.

"But I'll see you next weekend."

"I know, but seeing you at the show and having you at our house are two entirely different ball games. At least it looks like John got you and Herndon straightened out."

"I hope so. The show will tell."

Even before they unloaded the horse, DJ ran around the barn and up to Major's stall. Her whistle halfway there brought an answering whinny. He had his forehead against the bars, waiting for her when she trotted up. He snuffled her hair and her face and licked her hand. "I missed you, too, you big hunk of horsemeat. How you feeling, anyway?"

Ranger came to the corner of his pen and nickered for his share of attention.

"I'll be back. Just wait." DJ gave Major a last pat and ran back to unload Herndon and put him in his stall.

"Welcome back, you two," Bunny called. "Was awful quiet around here with you gone."

"Anything exciting happen?" Amy lifted DJ's saddle and bridle from the tack closet in the front of the trailer.

"Nope, not really. More kids riding since school is out. Bridget asked if I'd teach a beginner's jumping class, so that is new. For me, anyway."

"Good for you." Amy followed DJ and the horse into the barn.

DJ dumped Herndon's grain in the bucket and refilled his water. The hay manger was half full, so she left that. After petting him and checking to make sure the blanket was securely fashioned, they left him and headed up to Major's stall.

"See, he's putting weight on that foot."

Brad entered the stall and palpitated Major's shoulder, then ran his hands down the stoic horse's leg. "I don't feel any more swelling. Maybe you'll be able to turn him out to pasture soon."

"Robert said the pasture is all fenced now. He wants to run a water line out there so the horses always have water."

"Horses. You can't call General a horse." Amy rubbed Major's neck, too.

"Sure we can." DJ let Major scratch his forehead against her shoulder, then scrubbed the place for him with her fingernails.

"I better get going," Brad said. "Amy, you want a ride home or go to DJ's?"

"I need to get home before Mom starts to worry."

A few minutes later they pulled up in front of Amy's house. "Thanks for the ride and the great time this week," she said.

"Anytime. You ask your folks now if showing Western for me would be all right."

"I will." Amy piled her things beside the truck. "Thanks again."

"You know, you have one mighty good friend there." Brad pulled away from the curb.

"I know. I'm really lucky."

"Takes a good friend to have a good friend."

When DJ got home, Maria handed her several messages. DJ glanced down the paper and shook her head. "What happened?" The messages were all from card shops except for the one from Sean.

"Article come out in paper. You big success." Maria opened the drawer under the phone and handed DJ a newspaper article. "See."

DJ groaned at the picture of her and Amy and samples of their cards. They really looked like two kids playing grown-up. But the cards showed well. "Where's Mom?"

"All at Joe's. Back in time for dinner. You call there."

DJ did as ordered and heard the same information. She hung up and headed upstairs. She'd return the call to Sean before the others got home. But after leaving a message with his answering machine, DJ shook her head. More telephone tag. Between the two of them, talking on the phone almost took a miracle.

DJ started summer art school on Monday, but this time Gran took her.

"I want to see the art department and maybe meet your instructor," she said by way of excuse.

"You just want to sniff the paints and get your fingers in the clay," DJ said with a smile, but her butterflies were taking practice spins.

They parked in the north parking lot and followed the signs to the art department. "Mr. Charles said he didn't mind if I sat through the orientation. Makes me wish I could join you. I haven't played with clay for years."

"Why don't you?" DJ paused in the act of opening the door.

Gran stopped and looked at DJ. A smile started in one corner and soon widened her whole mouth, lighting up her eyes and even setting her silver hair to sparkling. "Why, darlin', why ever not?"

She left DJ seated for the lecture and came back half an hour later, admission slip in hand.

"Here." DJ handed her a supplies list.

Two hours later as they headed home, they were both digging clay out from under their fingernails and laughing about the trials of bringing up a form on the pottery wheel.

"I want to make some slab pieces, too. That kiln is huge." DJ dug at a piece of clay stuck to her jean shorts. "I wonder if I can make a horse statue by the end of the class?"

"I don't know why not. Or etch one on a piece of slab. Think how wonderful that could be. A horse etched in terra-cotta, or a bas-relief like that woman's face he showed us."

"Or I could carve it in more, you know, build up the

rump and shoulder . . ." DJ's fingers sketched the form in the air. She leaned back against the car seat. "And to think I get to do this every morning for six whole weeks."

"*We* get to, darlin', we get to."

Herndon behaved like an angel for the rest of the week so that DJ was actually looking forward to the show on the weekend. By the time she'd bathed him and braided his mane on Friday afternoon, he looked good enough to draw oohs and ahhs from the younger kids that idolized DJ.

But on Saturday DJ's butterflies awoke after a brief nap and went into full flutter as she trotted Herndon around the practice ring along with Tony and the other competing junior riders.

"You okay?" he asked. "Seems so strange to not see Major here."

"I know, but this guy has been on his best behavior today."

"Tell me about it. Two second-place ribbons and a third. And there's been hot competition here, too."

"I know." DJ swallowed hard. She and Herndon were the first ones into the ring for the jumping class.

"And now for the event you've been waiting for, junior jumpers, class number 43A on your programs. We have a good group of youngsters here today. We'll begin with number 16, owner and rider Darla Jean Randall on Herndon."

DJ smiled at Joe, who mouthed "Darla Jean" and made her smile. She swallowed, the gate swung open, and they cantered a circle and toward the first jump.

Over three and doing fine. DJ kept her gaze on the base of the brush jump in front of them. *Three, two, one, and* . . .

Herndon ran out.

Wanting to beat him, she brought him around again and headed for the jump. He ran out again. *If only we could fly over the stands and home without seeing or speaking to anyone.*

"All right, horse, behave yourself." Herndon took the jump. DJ gave a sigh of relief only to gather herself for the next one.

Herndon balked at the chicken coop.

DJ heard the announcer commiserating as she trotted her horse out of the arena. They were disqualified.

15

"I THINK I MIGHT HAVE TO SHOOT HIM. Or myself."

"Darla Jean Randall, what a thing to say." Brad laid a hand on her knee and squeezed.

"I second that." Joe stood on her other side.

DJ didn't dare touch her cheeks for fear she would burn her fingertips. "At least he didn't dump me."

"True, that's one good thing to be thankful for."

"I was so scared of him doing it that he probably read my mind." She could remember telling Amy she'd die of embarrassment if a horse ever did this to her. Ha, so she didn't die. She was still alive even though she wanted to burrow under the dirt and under the fence to someplace beyond the grounds before she came up for air.

Brad and Joe both looked up at her like she'd done something amazing. "I think you just hit the nail on the head, my girl. Did you tell John about that?"

"Tell him what? That horse can't read my mind."

"But he *can* read your body signals. Did you tell Bridget?"

DJ looked down at her grandfather. "You think I'd tell Bridget something like *that*?" Her voice squeaked on the final word.

Jackie stood on the other side of Brad. "DJ, you and I

need to have a serious discussion."

Herndon snorted and shifted. She felt like clobbering him. Jumping Major was so much easier.

"Well, let's get out of here." She knew she should wait and see Tony's round, but right now all she wanted to do was go home.

With Herndon loaded in the trailer, Jackie laid a hand on DJ's arm. "About that discussion?"

DJ made a face. "I know. You're going to say I should have told you or John or Bridget that, but I think I just figured it out for myself. How can I tell someone else when I don't know it?"

"Good point." Jackie gave her a hug. "But we want to make sure you know you can tell us anything. Anything, DJ, and we will do our best to help."

"I know." DJ scratched her ear. "Sometimes I think I am totally confused."

"Join the club. DJ, you've got to understand and remember: No matter what our emotion is—and fear is a strong one—our body communicates that with really subtle signals. Animals and some people are good at reading this."

"Well, if I'd understood it, I would have said something."

Oh really? her inner voice said with a devious chuckle.

"Mom, I think I need to go see Gran," DJ said after the family had returned from church the next morning.

"Sure. Is there something I can help you with?"

"Maybe, but . . ." DJ scrunched her mouth from one side to the other. "S'pose I better call and see if she's home, huh?" But Gran's phone rang until the answering machine picked up. DJ set the receiver back in the cradle. She didn't want to talk to an answering machine.

She couldn't settle in to finish another sketch of Stormy, either. And Amy had gone somewhere with her family. Maybe Joe and Gran were working outside and just didn't hear the phone.

"I'm going for a bike ride," she called. When no one answered, she stopped at the door to the garage. The house was amazingly quiet. From the deck she could hear the boys out at the barn with Robert. She took the stairs, but instead of going to her room, crossed to her parents' wing. She peeked in the door to see her mother sound asleep. Getting her bike out, she wheeled it out to the barn and told Robert she was taking a ride.

"Can we come?" The boys wriggled all over just like the dog between them.

DJ started to say no, but the pleading looks on their round faces did her in. "All right, but get your helmets."

"Where are you going?" Robert leaned on the shovel handle.

"To see if Joe and Gran are working outside. I called, but there was no answer."

"Is something wrong?"

Not if you don't include the fact that Herndon and I can't make it around the jumping arena without him running out on me. "No." She paused. "Yes, but I'm not sure what it is. I thought maybe Gran could help me sort it out."

"She and Joe are both good at that. If they're not home, why not come by and get me and I'll ride with you. Maybe we could go up to the Briones parking lot and up the trail."

"Okay." DJ took her helmet from the bars of her bike and set it on her head. With the chin strap latched, she rode back to where the helmeted boys were wheeling their bikes out of the garage. *This would be a good chance to start them on riding lessons.* She sent the thought flying. She had a feeling patience wouldn't be her strongest trait right then.

No Explorer in the driveway, no one answering their knock, no one working in the yard. The boys groaned, and DJ felt like groaning, too. But the ride up into the park cleared her head, and the antics of the twins made her laugh again.

The next day after school and lunch, DJ and Gran meandered out to the rose garden on the west side of Gran's house. Together they sank to their knees, pulling weeds with gloved hands and snipping off the dead blossoms.

"So what seems to be the problem?" Gran took a sniff of a creamy Peace rose and closed her eyes in delight. "Smell this."

DJ did and smiled back at her grandmother.

"Good, huh?"

DJ sighed and nodded. "I wish I knew what the problem was with my jumping Herndon." She dug out a dandelion and tossed it into the weed bucket. "I think I'm doing everything right, and still we get in trouble. Saturday I kind of said something offhand about being afraid." She glanced at her hand. "No, not about the fire thing, but about Herndon running out in public and embarrassing me to death. Do you think he could be picking up on that?"

Gran sat back on her knees. "Could be. Animals are terribly prescient." At DJ's questioning look, Gran smiled. "They can intuitively sense what we are feeling. Could be a smell, or small actions we aren't aware of, even facial expressions. Even though Herndon hasn't been with you very long, he could sense a quiver of fear."

"Hmm." DJ crossed her legs and rested her elbows on her knees.

"Why would his running out embarrass you so? I've seen it happen to lots of riders. They keep coming back, and they don't look like they are wearing a tattoo that spells idiot or some such."

"Just a permanent red face."

"Call it sunburn."

"I just don't trust him."

"Nor he you, it seems."

DJ nodded and picked a blade of grass. She nibbled the tender end of it while she thought. "Do you think any or all of my fears are connected somehow?"

"Another good question. I've been praying for God to help you deal with your fears, and recognizing them is always the first step. Maybe what's happening is you're beginning to recognize them."

DJ looked over at her grandmother. "I . . . I get so aggravated. With myself—why can't I get this? And with Herndon—why can't he behave like Major?" She shook her head. "I just don't get it."

"Remember, darlin', we prayed for wisdom for you, and I believe it is coming. You are doing some deep thinking and feeling and seeking. God honors our seeking hearts. And He loves you far more than you or I will ever understand. All we can do is live in His love and thank Him for it."

"I do—thank Him, I mean. Oh, not all the time, but more often than I used to. It's just this fear thing. He says not to be afraid."

Gran nodded. "He also says 'I love you' with an unending love and that we can take shelter in Him."

"I'm not sure I know how to do that."

"By taking time to sit and talk with Him. Picture yourself sitting at Jesus' knee, like you do mine." Gran smiled. "I tell myself that I am living in the shelter of God himself, and I keep saying it until I believe it."

"Cool, huh?" DJ rocked back, her hands clasped around her knees. "Way, way cool." She watched an orange-and-black butterfly flit from one rose blossom to another. She could hear bees buzzing about their business. Such perfect peace.

DJ tossed the blade of grass away as her feet hit the ground again. "It's silly to be afraid of being embarrassed because your horse might run out. If I'm going to be an Olympic rider, it will probably happen hundreds of times over the years."

"There, you've said it. No one ever died of embarrassment, at least not that I know of. Nor aggravation, either."

DJ grinned and tossed a blade of grass at her grandmother. "Thanks."

"You're welcome. Now, let's see if we can make a dent in the weeds here before you have to head for the Academy."

By the first of July Major had no trace of a limp. DJ called the vet in Palo Alto and told him the news.

"That's very good," Dr. Jones said. "I never expected him to recover this fast, if at all. He could very easily have limped for the rest of his life."

"Do you think I can ride him again?"

"I don't know why not, as long as you walk him first or put him on the hot walker for a while to see how he takes the exercise. I wouldn't try jumping him again."

"No, I didn't plan on that. But I know he misses the . . . the . . ." She wasn't sure what, but Major sometimes looked as if he'd lost his last friend when he saw her with Herndon.

"Have you let him out on pasture yet?"

"Yes, and he even gets down to roll."

"That's good news."

DJ hung up and ambled outside. Major stood with his

head over the fence, watching the boys play with General. The boys, the dog, and the pony spent more time together than anyone. They had taught General to bow down, and the sight of dog and pony bowing to a boy trying his best not to giggle made everyone laugh.

"He's jealous." DJ picked up her drawing pad and flipped the page from the drawing she'd been working on. "And he's just too big for the boys." Quickly she sketched in Major, trying for his dejected look. Then she flipped a page again and roughed in the four bowing to each other. Drawing people was much more difficult than drawing horses. Even dogs were easier. But at least she had the rough. She'd ask Gran to help with the boys. If she could make this work, it would look great in the card line.

When she bathed Herndon on Friday to get ready for the show, she felt that niggle of fear turn her stomach queasy again. Had that really been the problem? Her fear infecting her horse? *Guess we'll find out tomorrow.* She scraped him down and led him back to his stall, where she buckled his sheet in place and began braiding his mane.

DJ and Herndon had had a whole week of willing jumping. In the jumping arena at Briones, he sailed over the jumps with room to spare, even the odd ones that Bridget and Joe concocted to make him run out. Which was why DJ hadn't canceled their entry.

She had trouble going to sleep that night, but after praying for everyone and everything she could think of, she didn't check the time again. Until she woke up sweating, still hearing the horses screaming. A barn had been on fire again, and Major was trapped inside. Her face felt hot, like she'd been right next to the blaze, and her throat hurt like she'd been breathing smoke.

Still shaking, DJ got up and went to the bathroom for a glass of water. She chugged one full glass and refilled it, taking the glass with her back to bed. She sat on the edge of the bed, shivering and sipping. Thoughts of Major looking so sad wouldn't leave her alone. Major needed someone to fuss over him. But who?

The alarm went off an hour later. This time there was no dream, only heavy eyelids that didn't want to open until the sun came up. But juniors were up first this morning, and she had three classes, two of them jumping.

While her eyes didn't want to work, her butterflies didn't suffer that way at all. They were already fluttering up into her throat.

While Joe and Bunny carried on a lively conversation all the way to the show, DJ went back to sleep. Her apology when she woke up made them both laugh.

"I just figured you needed some extra sleep," Bunny said as she climbed out of the cab.

"You all right?" Joe asked.

"Sure. Thanks for letting me snooze."

While her butterflies kicked into full performance in the warm-up ring, DJ approached the entrance to the outdoor ring with a calm spirit—at least on the outside. If Herndon misbehaved, she'd try to figure out what she did wrong and not do it again. . . .

Nothing. If DJ didn't know better, she'd have thought she was riding a different horse. Herndon showed off like he'd been born for the ring. They'd taken a third in Open Equitation and a first in Hunter Seat. Now for the jumping.

"That should make you feel better," Joe said, smiling up at her and stroking Herndon's neck.

"It does, but we only got that because he's so showy."

"Not true. It takes two, and you did a good job out there."

"Thanks." She sucked in a deep breath. Junior Hunter

Over Fences was next. *"I can do all things through Christ who strengthens me."* She repeated the verse again and took in a deep breath. No fear. She thought of the verse Joe had given her earlier in the week. Something about God not giving a spirit of fear but of . . . She thought hard. Why had she had such a hard time memorizing it?

"Joe, what was that verse?" At his blank look, she began, "Not a spirit of fear but . . ."

Joe finished it for her. "But a spirit of power and love and self-control."

"Good."

"They're calling your number."

"I know." She took in another breath, smiled down at Joe, patted Herndon's neck, and trotted into the ring. She picked up a canter and circled toward the first jump. A simple post and rail, three feet high. *Come on, we can do this.* She could feel the power beneath her, indeed strength under control.

But what if I don't do it right?

Herndon's forward surge of power dropped, like someone had cut it right in half.

Like the shutter of a camera, she saw the click in her head. *That's it.*

Hands, legs, seat, *mind.*

DJ saw her stride. She squeezed her legs and felt her own strength return. *Hands, legs, seat, mind.* Herndon's power returned, just like throwing a light switch. *Three, two, one. Lift off.* Her arms followed up his neck. She could feel the surge of power as Herndon used himself to the fullest, his back rounded, DJ up over his withers where she belonged.

I'm with him! She wanted to shout it for all the world to hear. All other jumps had been only preparation for this. She could hardly keep from laughing out loud in sheer ecstasy.

Thank you, God!

She looked to the next jump, turning her head slightly to the right.

Herndon touched down on the right lead just like he needed to take the right turn and stride to the in and out. *Three, two, one.* And over. The other seven fences rolled under them as if Herndon could jump the moon.

The final jump looked huge, like a concrete wall three stories tall.

Herndon's ears pricked forward. He snorted. *Three, two, one*, and they sailed again. Higher he flew, clearing the four-foot jump by another foot.

They could have cleared a barn.

DJ couldn't quit laughing.

"The click, it happened! Did you see it? I can't believe it. That was the most awesome thing I've ever done." Words poured out of her, punctuated by bursts of laughter. "We did it!"

They took second place after two jump-offs, but DJ didn't care that they didn't get first. The sensation of control, of using her hands and feet the way she now knew she needed to. To ride this horse of hers like he deserved to be ridden.

"Thank you, thank you very much," she said to the ring steward as she accepted her ribbon. They trotted out the gate to a burst of applause. People on all sides of the arena shouted and clapped. Had their success been that obvious?

"You big handsome hunk of horseflesh," she said to his flickering ears and leaned forward to hug him.

"I hate to say I told you so, but . . ." Joe sported again.

"I know, you told me so." DJ dismounted and led Herndon over to the fence where her family stood, Gran included.

"DJ, you gots three ribbons today." Bobby held up two fingers on one hand and one on the other.

"Looked to me like you were having a good time out there." Robert, his arm around Lindy's shoulders, said with a smile.

"So was he." Lindy stroked Herndon's nose. "You are one handsome dude, you know that?"

DJ and Gran looked at each other, eyebrows disappearing in their hair. *Her* mother was not only talking to a horse but petting it. Without being coached.

A man who looked familiar waited just past the exit gate, next to Joe.

"Young lady, I just wanted to tell you congratulations. I've been watching you since your first show this year, and you've come a long way. I believe you have a real future in this sport if you keep working like you have been."

"Thank you." Only as he finished speaking did DJ put a face to the memory. The man who'd said she needed a decent horse.

Joe winked at her.

"I plan to keep on working hard." DJ watched him walk away. She sure did plan on continuing to work hard. They'd clicked; she'd gotten it. She finally understood what Bridget and John and Jackie had been talking about.

Wait until Bridget heard this story. If only she'd been here today. But more of the Academy kids were showing at another show, and she'd felt she needed to be there. Brad had missed it, too. What a story she had to tell.

"Joe, I've been thinking." They had unloaded the horses back at Briones and finished the evening chores. DJ slammed the truck door behind her. She and Joe ambled up the curved front walk to DJ's house, where all the others had gathered for a barbecue.

"Uh-oh, I know that tone of voice. What now?"

"You know, now that Shawna and her mom and dad are moved in . . ."

Shawna was DJ's nine-year-old cousin, daughter of Joe's younger son, Andy. They had bought DJ's old house.

"What do you think of me giving Major to Shawna? She's lighter and has no dream of showing and for sure not jumping. She needs a horse and Major needs . . ."

"Major needs to be needed. I think that's a fine idea. You can pasture him either here or at my house so you have him, too."

"I thought of that."

Joe put an arm around her shoulders. "Darla Jean Randall, you are one amazing kid—er, young woman, and I am proud to know you."

"Thanks, same to you."

"You've been letting go of a lot these last months."

"Yeah, right. Letting go of school, letting go of free time . . ."

"Smart aleck." He opened the door and ushered her in. "Hey, everybody, we're home."

"Billy, what happened to you?" DJ gasped at the sight of one of the twins.

"I let go too soon and fell off General." He put his hand to the goose egg on his forehead. "Daddy says I gots to hang on better."

DJ scooped him up in her arms and kissed his forehead. "So you've got to hang on longer, and I've got to let go sooner. Let's eat, I'm starved."

"And then we have fireworks." Billy put his palms on either side of DJ's face.

"I guess. What's the Fourth of July without sparklers? But you have to be careful."

Billy nodded. "We's always careful."

DJ shook her head and let him slide to the ground. "Yeah, right. And I'm Ronald McDonald." The three of them laughed their way into the house.